ONYEKA

AND THE RISE
OF THE REBELS

ONYEKA

AND THE RISE
OF THE REBELS

TỌLÁ OKOGWU

SIMON & SCHUSTER

First published in Great Britain in 2023 by Simon & Schuster UK Ltd

1 3 5 7 9 10 8 6 4 2

Simon & Schuster UK Ltd
1st Floor
222 Gray's Inn Road
London WC1X 8HB

www.simonandschuster.co.uk
www.simonandschuster.com.au
www.simonandschuster.co.in

Simon & Schuster Australia, Sydney
Simon & Schuster India, New Delhi

A CIP catalogue record for this book
is available from the British Library.

PB ISBN 978-1-3985-0511-7
eBook ISBN 978-1-3985-0512-4
eAudio ISBN 978-1-3985-0513-1

This book is a work of fiction. Names, characters, places and incidents are either
the product of the author's imagination or are used fictitiously. Any resemblance
to actual people living or dead, events or locales is entirely coincidental.

Typeset in Garamond by M Rules
Printed and Bound using 100% Renewable
Electricity at CPI Group (UK) Ltd

MIX
Paper | Supporting
responsible forestry
FSC® C171272

To God, to whom all the glory belongs.

CHAPTER ONE

I'm in a room. It's hot, dirty and cramped. There are no windows, and the only source of light is a naked bulb hanging from the centre of the ceiling. A red, black and green flag with half a yellow sun in the middle of it is attached to a wall. It looks similar to the flags that decorate the campus at the Academy of the Sun. On the floor near my feet is a single mattress where a small girl no older than six sleeps. Her dark coils rest against a stained sheet that used to be white, and the tattered blanket covering her rises gently as she breathes. She looks ill.

I'm waiting for someone, but I don't know who. I drop down to the mattress, my eyes drawn to the girl. A sheen of sweat covers her skin, but her face is relaxed as she sleeps. I reach out, running a light hand across her forehead. She's hot. Suddenly, her eyes open.

'I'm hungry,' she moans softly.

'I know, Chidinma,' I reply gently. I don't understand how I know this, or how I even know her name. I also know I have no food to give her and that we're running out of time.

Then a loud banging on the door shatters the silence and Chidinma stiffens.

'Stay here,' I whisper to her.

Chidinma nods and I head to the door. I take a deep breath and open it to reveal a teenage girl with hollow cheekbones – one of our neighbours from downstairs. My stomach tightens at the fear stamped across her face.

'The war is lost,' she says in an urgent voice. 'You should leave the village while you still can. There's a bus departing soon to take people to safety.'

I look back at Chidinma's weak body lying on the makeshift bed. There's no way she'd be able to walk.

'I need help,' I murmur quietly. 'My sister's sick.'

'We're all sick and hungry and tired,' the girl replies harshly. 'That's war.'

I grab her arm, desperate to make her listen. 'Please, I can't do this alone.'

Indecision crosses the girl's face, then she shrugs me off and marches back out.

Chidinma whimpers as I pull her into my arms. Her head lifts in a slow, painful movement. 'Is the war over? Did we win?' she asks.

I cradle her and begin to rock her in my arms. 'Yes. Everything will be fine.'

We both know I'm lying.

Suddenly, the dirty room and Chidinma melt away like smoke, and I'm alone in an empty place that feels lost to time. Where am I? Who am I? *Then a gentle hand touches my shoulder and I turn to find Dr Dòyìnbó beside me, his grey-flecked hair haloing his smiling face. I flinch, immediately reaching for Ike, but my power doesn't surface.*

Next to Dr Dòyìnbó, I notice a boy wearing an academy uniform. His face is turned slightly to the side, but I can see his expression is blank, almost as though he's not quite here. Something about him feels familiar though.

'Be calm. You're safe,' *Dr Dòyìnbó whispers.* 'But you must continue to serve Nigeria.'

His voice comes at me as if from a distance and I struggle to focus on it.

'What was that?' *I gasp.* 'Who's Chidinma?' *The image of the girl is still fresh in my mind.*

Dr Dòyìnbó blinks at me then glances at the boy, who says nothing. His eyes return to my face, examining me from head to toe like he's trying to figure out a puzzle.

'Well, this is unexpected,' *he finally says.* 'Who she is doesn't matter, Onyeka. It's what she represents that's important – an example of just one of the many different futures I've seen.'

'I don't understand.'

The smile he gives me is kind. 'I know you don't, but you needed to see what the future could have looked like so you can better understand why I've done all of this. Why I've been shaping this country and have used Solari to help me keep control of it.'

I turn away. 'I will never understand. You're a monster.'

Dr Dòyìnbó places a hand on my shoulder. 'I'm Nigeria's only hope. I've spent too many years creating the future you know, and I won't fail now.'

I spin back round. 'Yes, you will! Because I'm going to do everything I can to stop you.'

Dr Dòyìnbó sighs like I've disappointed him. 'See how the young speak. So certain, yet with barely any experience or knowledge to back up their words.' The hand on my shoulder tightens. 'Though you're right about one thing ... We're sure to meet again soon.'

Dr Dòyìnbó's eyes drill into mine. Pitch-black pools of determination stare back at me and a strangled scream crawls up the back of my throat—

I wake up suddenly, my stomach heaving as shallow breaths leave me in short, painful gasps. I feel like I'm going to throw up.

What was that?

It felt so real, almost as if it had actually happened. Then I remember Dr Dòyìnbó's words and understanding dawns. That wasn't just a dream I'd experienced; it was one of Dr Dòyìnbó's visions. It had felt stretched and faded, like an old shoe that Dr Dòyìnbó had worn too many times before. Only this time, he'd forced me to wear it. *But why?*

I rub my face. Even though I just woke up, I'm still tired. I'm always tired these days. My eyes move to the digital clock on the bedside table. It's almost eight in the morning and Adanna shifts in the bed opposite mine. We're roommates again, just like we were at the Academy of the Sun – the special school for genetically enhanced kids like us called Solari. Niyì and Hassan are Solari too. They're my friends, and along with Adanna, they make up the members of Nchebe. It means 'shield' in Igbo, and it's the collective name given to the most deserving JSS1 students at the Academy of the Sun who are tasked with defending the school. Although I don't even know if they can still call themselves Nchebe now.

Now that we've left the academy, there's no one to shield the remaining Solari from Dr Dòyìnbó and his terrible plan to take over Nigeria by using Solari as his soldiers. I shake my head quickly, trying to rid myself of thoughts of our old head teacher.

Adanna stirs again and I freeze until she goes still. I can barely make her out in the dim light of the room, but the steady rise and fall of her lumpy form reassures me and my body relaxes. The soft buzzing of a stray mosquito near my ear pulls me out of my thoughts and I slip out of bed. They were never a problem at the academy because of the repellent tech embedded across the campus. Here at the farmhouse, they're a total menace, but at least malaria is no longer a worry.

My feet move soundlessly as I make my way to the door, passing Adanna on the way. Her locs fan across her pillow, a dark contrast against the stark white fabric … *just like Chidinma*, the child in my dream. Adanna's face is creased into a tight grimace. A reminder that even in sleep, none of us can find any kind of peace. Not from the degenerative disease that kills Solari if they continue to use their powers, nor from the constant worry that Dr Dòyìnbó will find us now we know his true plans. With a final glance at Adanna, I quietly leave the room and head to the kitchen.

The open-plan living area of Aunt Naomi's farmhouse is simple. There aren't even any pictures on the walls, just like our house back in London … when Mum and I were in hiding. The housebot blinks at me as I pass its charging station. The automated robot does all the cleaning and small chores. Another light flickers – this time it's the motion sensor. There are several of them mounted around the house. Another reminder that we're not really safe.

A tiny wall gecko scurries past, its green speckled body clashing with the reddish-brown walls beneath its feet. I pass the orange sofa that Hassan likes to sink into when he's watching movies on the flat-screen TV that hangs above a stone mantel. Behind the sofa, a long, wooden bench marks the beginning of a surprisingly low-tech kitchen with mahogany cabinets. That's where you can usually find my aunt Naomi. She's my father's twin and a scientist too, although I only recently found out she existed. She's also always trying to feed somebody.

If Aunt Naomi's not in the kitchen, then you can usually find her in the lab in the basement. It's a replica of the one in

Lagos, where we first discovered how deadly the disease is and found out my father had created a serum to cure it. Up until then, we'd thought using Ike, the power all Solari have, caused mild sickness.

A power that will kill me soon ...

The thought flashes through my mind and I quickly push it away. It's been two weeks since we escaped from the Ogbunike Caves and Aunt Naomi brought us to the compound where her farmhouse sits, somewhere deep in the Rivers Province. It's one of the many places she used to hide from the Councils all those years ago after my father went missing, and it's where we're now hiding from Dr Dòyìnbó – the man who betrayed us. The man who knowingly exposed the citizens of Nigeria to trarium, an element he discovered, knowing it would cause mutations to their DNA.

The first few days were proper rough because we were so scared that we'd be found at any moment. But as the days went by and no one came looking for us, we settled into a strange sort of routine. Aunt Naomi even baked me a cake for my birthday last week. We all know it can't last, and that we need to go back to the Academy of the Sun eventually and face Dr Dòyìnbó, but so far no one's been able to come up with a plan we can all agree on. Aunt Naomi wants to go to the Councils that run Nigeria. She's sure they'll help us bring Dr Dòyìnbó to justice. Hassan thinks we should just storm AOS, which is what we call the academy. Adanna is adamant we need to find the Rogues, who are a group of Solari also trying to bring down Dr Dòyìnbó. And Niyì barely says anything at all, not since he lost his Ike.

It turns out my father's serum has a nasty side effect. It takes away our Ike. Niyì knew this when he stepped in front of a vacuum syringe full of the serum ... a syringe that was meant for me. Aunt Naomi has spent the last two weeks trying to get Niyì's Ike back, while also fixing the serum so we can cure our disease without removing Ike. She finally figured out the serum a few days ago, but we're waiting for her to be able to return Niyì's powers before we take it.

I heat up some Milo in the microwave and add three teaspoons of sugar. I need something sweet to take away the bitter taste of that vision. The cup has barely reached my lips when the door to my right swings open, revealing a tall boy. Niyì stands in the doorway, a haunted look on his face. It's the same look he's had since he lost his Ike. Niyì's skin is dull under the bright lights, and he rubs his face impatiently. He looks washed out, like a faded version of himself.

I give him a small welcoming smile. 'Couldn't sleep?'

'Something like that,' Niyì replies. It's still strange seeing him without Second Sight, the augmented reality glasses we all used to wear at the academy. That was another thing we had to get rid of so Dr Dòyìnbó couldn't track us.

I extend my mug to him, and Niyì reaches for it gratefully before taking a big gulp.

8

'Ergh ...' Niyì's mouth stretches into a disgusted grimace. 'How much sugar did you put in this?'

I frown back. 'Sorry. I had a bad dream.'

Niyì's face twitches. 'A dream?'

'Actually, it was more like a vision. It felt so weird.' I shake my head, trying to dislodge the memory of the child on the bed. I grab back my mug of hot chocolate and reach for a new one to make Niyì his own.

'Weird how?' Niyì's looking at me strangely now. His eyes are focused on me with a bright intensity.

The hairs on the back of my neck tingle. 'It had something to do with a war,' I reply slowly. 'Then there was a boy in an AOS uniform and ...' I look down, unable to continue. Unwilling to say his name.

'Dr Dòyìnbó was there too,' Niyì finishes, taking the new mug from me.

It feels odd hearing the name out loud. We've all been avoiding saying it for weeks. *Hold on ...* I lift startled eyes to Niyì's and an answering fear greets me.

'How did you know?' I whisper.

Niyì's hand tightens round his mug. 'I had the same dream too.'

CHAPTER TWO

'That's impossible,' I gasp and my hand drifts to the cowrie shell hanging from my neck. It's the key that unlocked my father's lab in Lagos and revealed the secret of the disease. It's also how I found out where he'd hidden the serum in Ogbunike Caves. My father always meant for me to have the shell, and my Aunt Naomi has a matching one.

'Wetin dey impossible?'

The question, spoken in Pidgin English, startles me and Niyì, and we both turn towards the new voice. Hassan shuffles sleepily into the kitchen. The lighter patch of skin round his right eye goes invisible for a moment as he rubs it tiredly. Aunt Naomi is always on at him for using Ike, but I don't think Hassan can help it. Just like he can't help slipping in and out of Pidgin.

'Na Milo be that?' Hassan says eagerly, spying the mug in Niyì's hand.

Niyì pulls the mug closer to him. 'Get your own.'

With a kiss of his teeth, Hassan sidesteps him and makes his way to the countertop.

'We had a dream about Dr Dòyìnbó,' Niyì says in a careful voice.

Hassan freezes, and his hand that's reaching for the canister of chocolate powder flashes invisible for a second. Then he swivels back round. 'Tósìn,' he whispers.

'You too, then?' Niyì asks.

Hassan nods and swallows. 'Yes o. E even wake me sef.'

'Dr Dòyìnbó's finally making his move,' Niyì says, his expression tightening.

The mug in my own hand begins to shake and dark brown liquid sloshes out. 'What are you talking about? What move? I don't understand!'

Niyì takes the mug from me and sets it down. 'We all had the same dream, which means it's not a coincidence. Dr Dòyìnbó must be using Tósìn to access us.'

Hassan's face creases into a frown and I stare between the two of them.

'Who's Tósìn?' I ask.

Niyì sighs. 'He's the boy we saw. He's a Solari at the academy who can manipulate memories and dreams.'

'Na lie!' Hassan bursts out. 'Tósìn no dey enter dream.'

'He can,' Niyì insists, and Hassan whistles between his teeth. 'Dr Dòyìnbó made him keep it a secret.'

11

My empty hand is trembling so much now. I clench it into a tight fist. 'You're saying Dr Dòyìnbó is using another Solari to hijack our dreams?'

Niyì nods and I swallow hard. It's bad enough that Dr Dòyìnbó has been letting Solari die, just so he can take control of Nigeria and fulfil his twisted visions of the future, but now he's invading our minds too. They're the one place that should be safe.

'But why?' I gasp.

'I think he's trying to convince us that Nigeria is doomed without him,' Niyì replies. 'If he's doing it to us, then I bet you he's dream-hacking everyone else at the academy too.' He taps the side of his head. 'Think about it – he needs Solari to be completely under his control, and now that *we* know his secret, time is running out.'

Niyì's words come to a rushed stop, and he looks away as if embarrassed. He's holding something back, I can feel it.

'How do *you* know about Tósìn and his powers?' I ask in a quiet voice.

Niyì's gaze swings back to mine. 'I used to get bad nightmares ... about Débò.'

I frown. When Niyì's ice powers first showed up, he accidentally used them on his best friend. He's been in a coma since. *But what does Débò have to do with this?*

'My dreams were becoming a distraction,' Niyì continues. 'So Dr Dòyìnbó got Tósìn to change them.' He slams his mug down, splashing Milo everywhere. 'It has to be Tósìn! It's the only explanation.'

A small shudder runs through Niyì, and he clasps his arms round his body as if he's trying to hold himself together. I caught Niyì watching us all a few days go as we played a game of Ayo round the kitchen table, his eyes following the clay seeds as they dropped into the pits of the wooden board game. But when I motioned for him to join us, he shook his head.

I still remember his expression. It was a mixture of envy and longing. He spends most of his time alone in the barn where we hide the Gyrfalcon, the super-sonic jet we used to escape Dr Dòyìnbó and his soldiers after they tried to steal the serum. Aunt Naomi says Niyì needs time to adjust, but I'm not so sure. When Niyì lost his Ike, it's like we lost him too, and I don't know how to get him back. It's even worse now that Aunt Naomi has fixed the old serum. *I don't want to lose any more people I love.*

I shut this thought down immediately . . . I can't let myself think about how Dr Dòyìnbó has my parents locked up somewhere. A bitter taste rises up the back of my throat, but I swallow the feeling. I can't lose control. I can't risk using Ike and setting off the sickness that always follows. It's so much worse for me because of how late my powers showed up, and because I kept using Ike when I didn't know about the disease, it has progressed too far.

Aunt Naomi has completely banned me from using Ike. She says if I don't take the new serum soon, it'll be too late. But it feels wrong to take it before we figure out how to return Niyì's powers. He lost them saving me, so I owe it to him. But I'm running out of time to find my parents and I'm going to need my Ike to do that.

'Who do you think the war was between?' Niyì asks suddenly. 'The neighbour in the dream,' he adds at my blank look. 'She said the war was lost.'

Hassan shrugs. 'Maybe na village or city?'

We all pause as we try to figure out what it could mean. The idea of Nigeria at war feels all types of wrong.

'Did Dr Dòyìnbó talk wit you for dream?' Hassan asks after a while.

Niyì nods and I breathe a sigh of relief that it wasn't just me Dr Dòyìnbó spoke to.

'He said Solari needed to serve Nigeria, but it didn't really feel like he was talking to me specifically.' Niyì shrugs, then his eyes flick to me. 'How about you, Onyeka?'

'Me neither.'

The lie slips from me before I can call it back. *Dr Dòyìnbó said my name.* I don't know why I'm covering up the truth, but seeing the way Niyì's face relaxes makes me glad I did. Besides, I don't want to worry anyone. I don't even know if there's anything to worry about yet.

'You tink Ada dream am too?' Hassan wonders.

If Adanna also had the same dream, there's only one way to find out. The three of us stare at each other nervously.

'No be me go wake am o,' Hassan finally hisses, backing away.

Adanna isn't a morning person, and the last time Hassan tried to wake her up, she threw her alarm clock at him.

I roll my eyes. 'Fine, I'll do it. But you'd better get Aunt Naomi too.'

Hassan nods eagerly, scrambling towards Aunt Naomi's room before I've even finished speaking. *Adanna isn't that scary.*

I make my way back to our bedroom and wake up Adanna, who immediately throws her pink Second Sight frames at me. She refused to ditch them, but they've been tweaked so no one at the academy can track them. After a few attempts and a ton of groaning, Adanna gets up and follows me into the open-plan living room. Aunt Naomi is already up and in the kitchen. Her tiny plaits swing as she chops up some peppers with the orange laser knife in her hand. The warm smell of akara hits me, and my belly rumbles in answer.

'This better be good,' Adanna grumbles behind me. 'I only just got back to sleep.'

'You had a nightmare, didn't you?' Niyì asks.

Adanna gasps and I turn round to find her mouth open like a startled fish. Then her eyes narrow.

'How do you know that?'

Niyì brings her up to speed. '... Aunt Naomi didn't have one, so I'm right in thinking that Dr Dòyìnbó's only targeting current students,' he finishes.

'But we're not at the academy any more,' I reply.

Adanna pushes her Second Sight further up her nose. 'Maybe it's a warning,' she says. 'That he can reach us wherever we go.' Her eyes get big. 'Maybe he knows where we are already?'

'I doubt it,' Aunt Naomi pipes up. 'The way I understand it, dream-hacking uses synaptic signatures based on exposure.'

There's total silence, and I reckon Adanna is the only one of us that understood anything my aunt just said.

Aunt Naomi sighs and her multi-coloured eyes flash as she puts the laser knife down. 'Basically, if Tósìn's been in physical contact with a person, he's probably been able to read their brain pattern. With that information, he can hack them from anywhere. But as far I know, it's a one-way connection, so he shouldn't be able to trace physical location. The fact you all shared the same dream would suggest we're safe.'

But my dream was different. Dr Dòyìnbó spoke to me directly. Still, I say nothing, uncertainty keeping the words trapped in my throat.

'To be on the safe side, I can teach you all a special trick to protect your minds.' Aunt Naomi flips some akara onto a plate before continuing. 'It's something I devised to prevent Onyeka's father from messing around with me when we were children. Our Ike, somewhat like Tósìn's, allows us to control minds, but it's possible to put up a mental shield to protect your mind from being accessed if you recognize the signs early.'

'How do we do that?' Niyì asks, reaching towards the plate of fried bean fritters.

Aunt Naomi bats his hand away. 'The second you feel someone trying to access your mind, you block them by using a special word. Then you empty your mind until only that word remains. The more you focus on it, the stronger your mental shield will be.'

It sounds a bit like the Fibonacci sequence my father taught me, and I say so aloud. Focusing on the sequence of numbers used to help me control my emotions.

'That's because your father stole the idea from me,' Aunt Naomi replies with a twist of her lips.

'But how do you know if someone is trying to get into your head in the first place?' I ask, still confused.

'It's a very specific sensation once you know what to look for – a foreign thing in the back of your mind, poking away at you. Like this . . .'

Aunt Naomi's voice trails off as her eyes narrow at me. Immediately, a strange sensation crawls into my mind. It feels like a searching finger, tracing an annoying pattern.

'Oh,' I gasp as understanding hits me.

'Build your shield,' Aunt Naomi commands.

There's a moment of confusion, but then I remember her instructions. Finding a word is easy: Nchebe. I fill my mind with the word until there's no other thought left. Slowly, the intrusive finger retreats and I smile triumphantly.

'Well done,' Aunt Naomi says with a strained smile. Using even a small amount of Ike wipes her out for hours. 'But

17

you should keep practising.' Then she turns to the others. 'All of you!'

The boys nod, but Adanna grabs a piece of akara, blowing on it hard. 'If there's even the smallest chance that Dr Dòyìnbó knows we're here, shouldn't we leave?' Every eye in the room turns to her as she takes a bite. 'What?' she says around a mouth full of food. 'It's the logical thing to do.'

'Where would we go?' Niyì asks in a biting tone. 'Logically, I mean.'

Adanna's eyes narrow, but she stays quiet. There's nothing to say, because there are no safe places any more. Not for us.

CHAPTER THREE

'Perhaps it's time we went to the Councils,' Aunt Naomi says quietly.

Hassan frowns as he loads up a plate of akara, and Niyì just snorts.

'We've been through this already,' he says. 'By the time we manage to get an audience with the Councils, Dr Dòyìnbó will have been alerted and he'll find a way to stop us.'

'Not if the Rogues help us,' Adanna replies, waving her fork at him. 'The Councils would have no choice but to believe all of us.'

'What if my father was wrong?' I whisper, voicing a very real worry. 'What if Gbénga is even worse than Dr Dòyìnbó?' No one has heard from the leader of the Rogues since he left the academy all those years ago. Since then, Dr Dòyìnbó has taught the Solari to think of him and the Rogues as traitors.

'And how are we supposed to find the Rogues anyway?' Niyì adds. 'You spend ages every day on that digital notepad we found in Onyeka's father's lab, and still we've got no new information.'

Adanna's been obsessed with fixing the corrupted data on the pad my father left for me to find in Lagos. It's how we learned about the disease in the first place. It's also how we discovered my father had been in contact with the Rogues and their leader Gbénga.

Adanna gives Niyì a death stare. 'I'm not going to give up when we know it's got all of Dr Uduike's research on it. Not to mention his messages to Gbénga.'

Niyì's glare is just as fierce. 'It's only useful if you can find it.'

'I could if I used Ike—' Adanna begins. Then she stops suddenly, her hand covering her mouth. 'I'm sorry, I didn't mean . . .' Her voice trails off in a helpless dribble.

A deafening silence fills the room. Since we arrived at the farmhouse, we've been avoiding talking about Ike and we've tried not to use it either. After what happened to Niyì, it feels wrong to call on our powers.

'We all agreed to wait until Aunt Naomi returns Niyì's Ike,' I hiss, throwing Adanna a sharp look.

'It's fine,' Niyì mutters, then he takes a deep breath. 'I think we should go back to AOS and convince the other Solari to help us, before it's too late.'

'It's already too late,' Adanna mutters, and all eyes turn to her. 'I was checking AOSnet yesterday.'

Niyì releases a loud breath. 'You said you wouldn't go on it any more!'

'I know, but it's the only way to track what's going on at the academy.'

'What if you get caught?' Niyì says. 'What if Dr Dòyìnbó tracks us here?'

'I'm being careful.'

Niyì glares at her, and Adanna stares back with her own stubborn expression. They're about to kick off again, I can feel it.

'Wetin you find?' Hassan asks, trying to distract them before they really get going.

Adanna hesitates for a second before continuing. 'Dr Dòyìnbó issued a school-wide bulletin declaring us Rogue spies. He's telling everyone that we betrayed our friends, our school and our country.'

Niyì's face falls. 'What?'

'I guess he had to come up with an explanation for our disappearance,' Aunt Naomi says.

'You should see the comments under the bulletin,' Adanna mutters. 'Ẹni and her friends are having a blast.'

It's hard to miss the pain in Adanna's voice. She's spent years fighting to be accepted at AOS after Ẹni, her former roommate, spread jealous lies about her being a Rogue spy. We thought winning Ìdánwò, the inter-house tournament would help, but now Dr Dòyìnbó has just gone and backed Ẹni up. I can hardly believe Ìdánwò was just a few weeks ago. It felt like the most important thing back then, and I'd give anything to go back to that simpler time.

If Dr Dòyìnbó is lying to the Solari about us, he's probably lying to the Councils too, so there's no way anyone will believe us now. It feels as if the walls are closing in as all our options disappear like the akara did from our plates. Dr Dòyìnbó is too powerful and we're just kids.

An overwhelming swell of fear rises in me, rushing through my body until I'm almost vibrating with the intensity of it. I try to keep a lid on it because it isn't safe for me to feel this much emotion, but it's too late. The horror of Dr Dòyìnbó's vision and the hopelessness of our situation finally crumbles my defences.

'It's not fair,' I gasp as tears fill my eyes.

'Uh oh,' Adana mutters. 'She's losing control again.'

'We're not traitors,' I sob.

I'm a volcano that's been asleep too long. The red-hot emotions that have been brewing since we discovered the truth about Dr Dòyìnbó erupt in my belly.

He lied about not being a Solari.

He betrayed us so he could turn Solari into his own personal army and take over Nigeria.

He took Niyì's Ike.

He has my parents!

It's all too much and I don't know how to carry the weight of it any more. The last of my barriers dissolve, and with nothing left to hold it back, Ike rises up immediately. It prickles a painful path across my scalp as a bolt of my hair whips out, smashing into one of the kitchen cabinets and splintering the solid wood.

'Onyeka!' Adanna hisses, and my scalp thrums in response to the anchoring pull of her voice. 'You've got to calm down.'

I'm beyond listening though. 'We're never going to find my parents.' My voice is a broken wail as my fear and pain spills over.

Another bolt of hair whistles through the air, this time knocking over the kettle. Hot water leaks from it, like the tears spilling down my face. Aunt Naomi gasps and Hassan stares at me with a look of helpless worry. Niyì's face is blank. I can't read him these days.

Adanna leans in close. 'We'll figure it out, I promise. But first you need to focus on the four of us to help you calm down.'

'What she needs is the new serum,' Niyì growls. 'There's no point waiting any more.'

'No!' I pant, his words pushing through my panic. 'Not until we fix you.'

Niyì flinches and looks away. A wave of nausea hits and, at the same time, pain rips through my head. I wince at the intensity of it. This is the worst the sickness has ever been, but we have to hold off on taking the serum. I know Aunt Naomi said she'll keep working on restoring Niyì's Ike, but we should *all* be able to use our powers together. It isn't fair otherwise.

'Focus on us,' Adanna tries again. 'Focus on our connection.'

She grabs my hand and gives it a squeeze, but it's not enough. My connection to her and the others as my anchors has been strained since we got to the farmhouse, and I can barely focus on it past the pain.

Hassan frowns. 'E no dey work o.'

'This is stupid.' Niyì turns to Aunt Naomi. 'She needs to take the serum, and fast!'

Aunt Naomi nods and moves away, disappearing down the corridor that leads to the lab. I know immediately what she's doing. I also know that Niyì's right and I've run out of time. But it still feels wrong.

It doesn't take long for Aunt Naomi to return with a vacuum syringe in one hand and four vials filled with clear liquid in the other hand. She quickly loads one of the vials into the syringe, then drops down beside me. Her eyes meet mine, pleading silently for understanding ... for permission. I turn to Niyì, but his face is blank again.

I nod and Adanna grabs my arm as Aunt Naomi presses the syringe into it. At first, I feel a firm pressure, then a cold heat spreads up my arm. As the freezing burn races through my body, the pain and nausea retreat, chased away by the power of the serum now rushing through my system. My hair subsides, but I can still feel the raw power of my Ike bubbling under the surface of my skin.

'I'm not in pain any more,' I whisper.

'That's a good sign,' Aunt Naomi replies. 'Can you try to use your Ike?'

I struggle to find an emotion to fuel my Ike at first. Where there should be joy, I find only guilt churning inside me because of Niyì.

With no other choice, I tap into the emotion reluctantly and immediately my hair flares up around me again. Adanna and Aunt Naomi step back as the halo of coils swirls in the air in a happy dance. There's no prickling pain, not even the nausea I've become so used to whenever I use Ike. Before I can stop it, a small laugh escapes my mouth.

Aunt Naomi's lips curve up in a relieved smile. 'I'll still need to run some additional tests, but I'm fairly certain the serum has worked as expected.'

'So, na our turn?' Hassan asks.

Aunt Naomi glances at Niyì. His expression is tight, like he's trying to hide his true feelings, and my heart sinks.

'If we're going to take down Dr Dòyìnbó, we need to be ready,' Niyì mutters. 'We can't wait any longer.'

No one argues this time and, within moments, the remaining three vials of serum are inside Hassan, Adanna and Aunt Naomi. Nothing happens at first, then Hassan stretches out a hand and a yellow energy field bursts from it.

'I feel amazing,' he breathes, switching to English.

Suddenly, the TV blinks awake and music spills from the integrated sound system. I spot the satisfied grin splitting

Adanna's face. She must have used her technopath power. I guess this means she'll also be smelling and hearing our emotions again. Adanna's a synaesthetic empath too. I'm not sure I miss that particular Ike. I smile at the both of them, though, glad that we have one less thing to worry about.

But when I look at Niyì, the expression on his face freezes the smile on my mine. Longing blazes back at me, and I suck in a sharp breath. Niyì catches me and flinches, then he spins away, heading towards the double glass doors that lead to the barn. I move to follow when a hand on my shoulder stops me.

Aunt Naomi shakes her head. 'Leave him. He needs some space.'

A heavy weight settles in my belly as Niyì retreats from us. This is what I was worried would happen. This is why I wanted to wait. We should all be celebrating right now, but what little joy there is evaporates as Niyì moves further away into the distance.

CHAPTER FOUR

I wake up the next day to the buzzing of Adanna's alarm and the sound of rain hitting the bedroom window. I crack open one eye, ready to finish her for waking me up, but then I realize it's my phone. When we first arrived at the farmhouse, Aunt Naomi gave each of us special encrypted devices. They're pretty basic, but at least we can send text messages from them. I grab mine and see a message from my best friend, Cheyenne, who's back in London. I texted her late last night and she must have only just seen it.

How are u feelin now? Is everyone okay? How's Niyì?

I grimace, then begin typing.

I'm good. Sickness is completely gone.

It's true. This is the best I've felt since my powers first showed up.

Niyì is ...

My fingers still as I try to find the words to explain how he is.
In the end I settle for

fine.

That's great. What's the next move? Any closer to finding
ur parents?

My heart sinks when I read her last question. Chey's the only
person that doesn't worry they'll upset me if they talk about my
parents. In a way, I'm glad. As hard as it is to think about them,
it helps me stay focused on finding them.

We're still figuring some stuff out, but we've got this

I wish I was there with u

I wish she was too. Cheyenne has a way of making even the
hardest things seem possible. But no matter how much I want
to see her, it's way too dangerous.

Like u'd miss ur art camp just to come here!

28

> For u I would, but no lie, it would be hard :)

She means it. Cheyenne's parents signed her up to a special art camp in Birmingham, and she's been looking forward to it for months.

> When do u leave?

> A few weeks. I'm well ready. No school and no parents for a whole week

I laugh and Adanna stirs in the bed next to mine.

'You're texting Cheyenne, aren't you?' she says sleepily, then rolls back over. 'Say hi for me.'

> Ada says hi

> Tell her I'm going to crush her next time we play Battlestar Ninjas. Gotta go. TTYL

> Ha! I'm not getting involved in ur gaming beef. Laters

With a sigh, I throw the phone down on the bed and get up. Each day is pretty much the same here. It's filled with a whole load of waiting and arguing about what we should do next. Today should be different after what happened yesterday, but I don't know if it will be. Niyì spent the whole day avoiding all of us, while Aunt Naomi and Adanna were busy in the lab. That just left me and Hassan killing time by playing video games and watching movies, but I ended up having to listen to him snore throughout most of them.

Niyì doesn't turn up for breakfast with everyone else, and when he also misses lunch, I decide he's had enough space and finally go looking for him. I don't have to look very hard though. I just follow the sound of BuzzChild, the latest Afrobeat star, outside to the barn. It's raining, but the air is still hot as I dash across the hard ground, which is typical weather in Nigeria during October. An agama lizard blinks at me as I pass a big orange tree, its bright orange head bobbing along to the music. The tangy scent of the fruit hits me, and I try to imagine the grey cold of London, but it's getting harder to remember it as each day passes.

I find Niyì inside the Gyrfalcon. The jet has been pretty much grounded since we arrived as we rarely leave the farmhouse. The only time we take it out is so we can charge the solar batteries, but we always turn on stealth technology, which allows us to hide our presence while in the air. Aunt Naomi gets all the shopping delivered via delivery drones. Niyì still checks on the Gyrfalcon every day though, tinkering with machinery I don't understand.

This time, he's fiddling with one of the buttons embedded in the control panels. The bright backlight reflects on his face, making his skin look even more grey than usual.

'Hey,' I call out hesitantly. 'You missed breakfast and lunch.'

Niyì shrugs.

'Aunt Naomi made pepper soup,' I offer. 'It's your favourite.'

'I'm not hungry,' he says flatly.

I sigh at the disinterest in his voice. It's how he sounds most of the time now.

'Do you want to talk?' I probe.

'About what?'

'I dunno.' I shrug. 'Anything.'

He doesn't even look up. 'Not really.'

'Seriously?' I snap, finally losing patience. 'What happened yesterday was huge. You must feel some kind of way about it?'

Niyì looks up at me then, and I flinch at the faraway look in his eyes. 'Did you know that during my first year at the academy, I wished every day that my Ike would disappear.'

The change of subject startles me.

'N-no,' I stutter. 'Why?'

'It felt like a curse. I lost my best friend, my parents and my home because of it.' His voice trails off as a shudder runs through him.

'Niyì.' I step closer and place a tentative hand on his shoulder.

He blinks, as if seeing me properly. 'I was six years old when Dr Dòyìnbó found me and brought me to the academy.' His voice is as empty as his eyes, and my hand drops back down to my side. 'He made me believe that I was special.' Niyì stares down at the floor. 'He helped me realize that Ike is a gift, and I could use it for good.' Then he spreads his arms wide. 'And now it's gone.'

This is my fault. I stay silent as the thought runs through my mind. Niyì lost his Ike trying to protect me. No matter how hard I try, I can't seem to shake the heavy guilt that continues to weigh me down.

A strange emotion burns behind Niyì's eyes. 'Dr Dòyìnbó gave me a new home, a family and a future. Now all that's gone too.'

'No, it's not!' I tell him. 'We're still your family. We'll get your Ike back and we'll stop Dr Dòyìnbó.'

'How?' Niyì replies with a twist of his lips. 'We can't even agree on a plan, so tell me how we're going to stop him.'

My shoulders droop. He's right, but I'm not ready to give up. Too much depends on it. My shoulders straighten again. 'I'll figure it out,' I reply with determination.

A blazing fury enters his eyes. 'We're running out of time and options. I'm useless in this state, and eventually you're going to have to leave me behind.'

I look away. 'We're not leaving anyone behind.'

'We left the others at the academy behind.' I stiffen at the harsh words. 'Face it, Onyeka, we can't beat him. Dr Dòyìnbó is too powerful.'

'I don't believe that,' I murmur on a shaky breath as my hands lock together. 'We can still fix everything.'

'You can't fix this, Onyeka!' he yells, and I take a startled step back. Niyì's eyes widen, and he rubs a hand over his face. 'You can't fix me.' His voice is barely a whisper this time.

He's wrong. He has to be. Maybe now the sickness is gone, Adanna can use her technopath powers to help Aunt Naomi find a way to get back Niyì's Ike. I tell him all of this, but he looks away and says nothing.

I sigh. Aunt Naomi was right. I should have just left him alone. But doing that wasn't working either. The more space we give him, the more distant he becomes, and it feels like we're losing him.

'You're wrong,' I say quietly. 'I know you don't believe it right now, but we're going to make everything right again.'

Niyì looks at me then. 'Even if we get my powers back, I don't have an anchor any more.'

'Are you sure?' I reply. I'd been thinking about this a lot. Every Solari needs something to stabilize their emotions so they can use Ike properly, and I'd always suspected Dr Dòyìnbó might be Niyì's anchor. 'I know Dr Dòyìnbó meant a lot to you, but doesn't the academy mean more? Think about it.'

Niyì's face scrunches up, as if he's considering my words, and a spark of hope races through me. *Maybe I'm finally getting through to him*. But then he frowns.

'It doesn't matter anyway.'

With those words, Niyì turns back to the screen in front of

him, his face once again a blank mask. The spark of hope dies, and I leave him to it.

'He's acting so strange.'

I close the door behind me as I enter my room and I throw myself onto Adanna's bed. My father's digital pad resting beside Adanna bounces once, but she doesn't even flinch. Her eyes are glued to an unfamiliar device resting in her lap as her fingers tinker with it.

'For solar's sake. Is Hassan still being a big baby?' Adanna mutters. 'Tell him I'll replace his bag of chin chin later.'

I wrinkle my nose at her. Hassan is obsessed with the sweet crunchy snack, but I'm not bothered about that right now.

'I'm talking about Niyì.'

Adanna's fingers pause. 'Oh.' Then they resume their wild dance.

Is she even listening?

'Ada?' I try again.

Her eyes finally leave the wand-like device before she turns to me with an impatient look. 'I'll never get this holomorpher finished if you keep disturbing me. Besides, if you lost your Ike, wouldn't you be acting strangely too?'

That shuts me up, but only for a second. 'He's acting like there's no hope left.'

'He's in pain and he's sad, Onyeka. You both are.'

I push off the bed, moving into a seated position. 'What do you mean?'

Adanna tilts her head at me. 'You do realize I can once again use Ike any time I want. In fact, without the constant headache, I'm even better at reading emotions now.'

'Don't you dare,' I reply with a warning frown.

'Too late,' she says with smug grin. 'All that guilt you're carrying around sounds like a whole orchestra.'

'I don't know what you're talking about.'

Her left eyebrow lifts. 'You really want to play that game with me?'

I try to stare her down, but my eyes drop away after a few seconds. I swallow hard, trying not to bawl the way I want to.

'I feel like everything is my fault.' The words spill from me unexpectedly – forbidden thoughts that I haven't dared let myself say aloud since everything fell apart two weeks ago. 'I fell for Dr Dòyìnbó's lies and, without me, we wouldn't be in this mess.'

Adanna sighs. 'Why are you trying to take all the guilt for yourself?' I frown at her, and she puts down the strange device. 'I trusted Dr Dòyìnbó too. Does that make it my fault as well?'

'No, but . . .' I begin, but my voice trails off uncertainly.

Adanna places her hand over mine. 'Doesn't make much sense, does it?'

In my heart, I know she's right, yet I can't shed the layer of doubt that remains. Because she's a total know-it-all, Adanna's hand tightens over mine.

'Niyì made his choice, and I know he'd do the same thing again.'

Her words speak to my deepest fears, and my heart begins to race, an irregular rhythm thumping in my chest.

'What if you're wrong? What if he regrets saving me?' I whisper back.

'I can sense emotions, remember? Niyì is a Protector. He doesn't know how to be any other way.'

'But that's the problem!' The words erupt from me, and once they're in the open, more rush out like a river bursting its banks. 'Niyì's been training to be a Protector for so long that it's become who he is. So what happens if we can't get his Ike back?'

Am I about to lose someone else I care about? I don't say this last part out loud, but from the way Adanna's looking at me, I can tell she sensed it anyway.

Adanna releases my hand. 'I don't know, but we'll figure it out together.' Then she picks up the digital pad. 'Besides, I think I've finally figured out how we get out of this mess.' She waves it in front of me. 'Before you and your emotions decided to disturb me, I finally pieced together a message from Gbénga to your father.'

I blink at her. I wasn't expecting that. That's when I notice her locs are down – a sure sign she's been working in the lab again.

'What are you talking about?'

'Look, here's an email between Dr Uduike and Gbénga.' Adanna pushes the pad towards me with a grin. 'They were talking about Dr Dòyìnbó's plans.'

'Oh . . .' I say, excitement beginning to build.

Adanna's grin is even wider now. 'I found something else too. Something big.'

CHAPTER FIVE

Adanna wouldn't tell me what she'd found until everyone was gathered together in the lab in the basement. It's not as big as my father's lab in Lagos, but it has newer, better tech. Lights flash from all sorts of equipment that only Aunt Naomi and Adanna are allowed to touch. Adanna quickly fills the others in about the email she discovered.

'Na wa o,' Hassan exclaims, staring at Adanna's smug face. 'So that pad no dey useless again.'

Adanna cuts her eyes at him. 'It's you that's useless,' she replies, before cradling the tablet close. 'I found a phone number,' she adds triumphantly.

'You've found a way to contact the Rogues?' I gasp.

Adanna nods as her lips creep up into a slow smile. 'It's over ten years old, but it's a starting point.'

She presses a button on her computer and a 3D map of

Nigeria flashes up in the air in front of us. It looks like the one Professor Sàlàkọ́, our history teacher back at the academy, likes to use. The virtual map shifts, zooming into a specific city with tall buildings and dome-topped mosques.

'What are we looking at?' I ask.

Adanna grins, twin dimples flashing her glee. 'Kano.'

Hassan straightens. 'Why we dey go Kano? You know say na my hometown.'

I glance at Niyì, who's standing brooding by one of the tables. That's the kind of question he would have asked in the past. Now he just looks bored as the map zooms into a precise location.

'The Rogues,' Adanna announces victoriously. 'I managed to trace the phone number from the email. It's linked to what looks like an abandoned compound just outside Kano.'

The angle of the map shifts, focusing on a series of flat, rectangular buildings.

'I couldn't find any current records of ownership,' Adanna continues. 'But I did find an old mail redirection for Mr G Ìdánwò.'

A hush descends on the room as we all stare at each other. Only Solari who've been at the academy know that the annual house tournament is called Ìdánwò.

'So, what do we do now?' Aunt Naomi asks. She's been pretty quiet so far. Come to think of it, she's been quiet since we took the serum yesterday. I figured she was getting used to being able to use her Ike freely again. I can't even imagine how she must feel after so many years of having to deny such a big part of herself.

Adanna throws her a confused look. 'What do you mean? We have to check it out, of course.'

'Really?' Niyì sneers. 'You think the Rogues will still be there after all this time? Even after Onyeka's dad was kidnapped? That doesn't make any sense.'

Adanna places the tablet down onto the nearest table. 'I don't see you coming up with any useful ideas.'

'Fine, if you must know, I think we should take back the academy,' Niyì says, crossing his arms.

'Well done,' Adanna sniffs. 'Let's go and get ourselves captured by storming AOS. Brilliant plan, Niyì.'

'This isn't helping,' I remind them both, and Hassan nods, backing me up.

'I agree with Niyì about the Rogues,' Aunt Naomi cuts in quietly. 'We can't go charging into Kano either. Not without being sure what's there or if we're welcome.'

With one last dirty look at Niyì, Adanna picks up the pad again. 'I'm still working on verifying the number. I've got an advance search running on it.'

'Make we just call the number?' Hassan asks.

Adanna stares at him like it hadn't occurred to her to try that.

'It's not a secure line,' she splutters. 'Anyone could be listening in.'

'It could also be a trap,' Aunt Naomi offers. 'Have you thought about that?'

Adanna goes silent, and I can tell she hasn't, which isn't like her. She's usually the first to spot the holes in everyone else's ideas.

'How do we even know Gbénga will help us?' I ask gently.

She glares at me. 'Because your father said he would.'

It's my turn to shut up. So far, everything my father said has been true. But really, I know nothing about him. We thought we knew Dr Dòyìnbó, and look what he did to us. Four pairs of eyes stare at me like they're waiting for me to make the decision. But it isn't just mine to make.

'Hassan?' I ask.

He frowns at the map still hovering in the air and shakes his head. 'We go need help o.'

Aunt Naomi sighs, then nods. I can already feel Adanna's excitement, so I don't bother asking her. I turn to Niyì instead.

'What do you think?'

Niyì's eyes narrow. 'The Solari at the academy need us.'

He's right, but so is Adanna. We're not strong enough to take on Dr Dòyìnbó. Even if Niyì had his Ike, we'd still need help. Something in my face must give me away, because Niyì's eyes drop, his disappointment clear.

I make my decision.

'I think we should go back to the academy.'

Niyì's eyes swing back to mine in bug-eyed disbelief. Adanna stares at me with a matching expression.

'But—' she begins.

Adanna doesn't finish though as a loud siren blares through the lab. Aunt Naomi scrambles towards a panel embedded in the wall. Her fingers flying as she types in a series of numbers.

'Someone's breached the perimeter defences,' she finally mutters.

We all stare at her. I didn't even know the farmhouse had perimeter defences.

'Who is it?' Niyì asks.

'I can't tell yet, but they're armed and fast,' Aunt Naomi replies, concern creeping into her voice as she watches something on the small viewscreen beside the keypad.

'It has to be Dr Dòyìnbó,' Adanna whispers, adjusting her Second Sight with a shaking hand. 'Who else would be looking for us?'

Aunt Naomi's face looks strained. 'Well, whoever it is, they'll be here soon.'

'Wetin we go do?' Hassan starts flickering in and out of view, and I feel my eyes cross as I try to keep track of him.

'The Gyrfalcon,' Niyì says in a firm voice. 'It's prepped and ready to go.'

Aunt Naomi grabs a bag from one of the cupboards and starts stuffing papers and other things I don't recognize into it.

'What are you doing?' I ask her. 'We don't have time for this.'

She doesn't stop. 'We can't just leave all this data here. It's too dangerous if it gets into the wrong hands.'

'She's right,' Adanna says from behind me. Then sparks light up the room as a computer next to her explodes.

'Chai!' Hassan squeaks. 'Wetin happen?'

'I'm frying the computer hard drives. It's not foolproof, but it's all we've got time for.'

Adanna closes her eyes, and another hard drive explodes with a bang. Soon the lab looks like a firework display gone wrong. Wires fly across the room as Aunt Naomi's expensive equipment disintegrates and a big grin spreads over Adanna's face. I didn't know she liked blowing things up so much.

'We don't have time for you to destroy all of them,' Aunt Naomi shouts. 'We have to leave now. They're almost here.'

She leads the way out of the lab, and we rush back up the stairs. The kitchen looks just as it did at lunch. The housebot was supposed to clear everything away, but our plates still line the tabletop, pieces of cold meat hardening by the sink. Fresh sunlight streams through the rain-spattered windows as we head for the glass doors at the back of the farmhouse. It's a straight path from there to the barn and the safety of the Gyrfalcon.

Even though we've all been waiting for this time to come, it's still hard to believe that Dr Dòyìnbó has finally found us. *We're not ready!*

Then there's a sudden loud bang and glass goes flying everywhere. Dense smoke fills the air.

'Get down,' Niyì screams as the remaining windows break with a crash.

I hit the floor, pulling Adanna down with me. The smoke thickens, making it difficult to see … to even breathe. The intruders have arrived, and they've come prepared.

'Can you see anyone?' Adanna whispers urgently beside me.

I shake my head before I realize she can't see me through all the smoke.

'No,' I whisper back. 'We need to keep moving.'

'How? It's too smoky in here.'

She's right. But I can fix that. Using the panic racing through me, I call up my Ike and anchor it quickly. I stand as my hair lifts around me, separating into two thick ropes. I let them rise into the air above my head and they start to spin, slowly at first, then building up speed until they whirl above me like a giant fan.

The smoke begins to lift, sucked up by the vacuum created by my hair, and familiar furniture once again becomes visible. Soon, I can see walls and shattered window frames where glass once sat. Then I spot a dark figure where the front door used to be. I don't hesitate, and a bolt of hair whips out, knocking the figure aside like a bowling pin. But they're not alone. More appear at the door and windows dressed in the same green camouflage uniforms as the soldiers who attacked us in my father's lab weeks ago. Their faces are covered by thick, black breathing masks.

Niyì, Hassan and Aunt Naomi are close to the back doors,

and they stand now, ready to face the invaders. Adanna is up too, crouched in a defensive position. My eyes meet Niyì's. He's never had to fight without his Ike before. Even though Ms Bello, our PE teacher at AOS, taught us to defend ourselves without using it, we always knew we could call on it if we needed to.

If things get bad now, Niyì won't have that safety net. I shake my head at him, hoping he listens and stays back. His face tightens and his stance shifts, falling into the strike position Ms Bello drilled into us. *I guess that's that.*

'The plan hasn't changed,' he calls out, sounding like his old self again. 'We just have a new problem to solve.'

His voice acts like a starter gun, and the soldiers charge at us. I pull my hair back like a whip, ready to deal with the first person who even looks at me wrong. Everything slows down as a soldier nears, and I feel anticipation rise in me. Then a sharp voice rings out.

'SLEEP!'

The soldier charging towards me freezes mid-stride, his head cocked to the side in disbelief. Then he crumples to ground like a puppet whose strings have been cut. He isn't the only one. Every other soldier falls too, hitting the ground in a collective thud that sounds like a slap.

'We don't have time for this,' Aunt Naomi says, breathing heavily.

A fine sheen of sweat glistens on her forehead, just like it did when she last used her Ike.

'Let's move,' Niyì calls.

We file out of the broken glass doors that lead outside. The air is the humid kind you get just after it's rained, and we sprint across the damp ground towards the big wooden doors of the barn. We don't get far though as three figures step out of the shadow of the big tree near the barn. They come to a stop, blocking our way.

I recognize the first figure immediately. Ẹni's violet headtie flutters in the light wind, matching the rest of her House Transformer uniform. A smug grin is plastered across her face. To her left is a boy dressed in the blue of House Psionic. Fọlákúnlé's oiled twists gleam under the bright glare of the sun, and round his neck is a thin, gold necklace he never takes off. He's in the same year and house as me and Adanna, but we've never hung out. The sight of the second boy to Ẹni's right makes me freeze.

Òrẹ́'s deep black eyes stare back at us. I haven't seen him since he helped me and Adanna beat Ẹni in Ìdánwò. *What is he doing here?* I can't read his expression, but everything about his body language says he'd rather be anywhere else.

Ẹni steps forward then, a grim smile playing on her lips. 'By order of Dr Dòyìnbó, you're to return with us to AOS to answer for your crimes.'

CHAPTER SIX

Nobody moves. It's as if we've been frozen by her ridiculous words. Then Adanna starts laughing. I glance at her from the corner of my eye. *Is she all right?*

'Did it feel good saying that?' Adanna finally splutters.

Ẹni frowns. 'Did you hear me? You're to come with us.'

'Yeah, that's not going to happen,' Adanna replies.

'I always knew you were a Rogue spy,' Ẹni sneers. 'And now everyone else knows it too.'

Adanna's laughter stops immediately. 'That's a complete lie. We're not Rogue spies.'

'That's not what Dr Dòyìnbó says.' Ẹni's the one smiling now.

'Forget what he said,' I cut in. 'Dr Dòyìnbó's been lying to everyone about Ike, about who he is and even his plans for Solari.'

Ẹni throws me an unimpressed look. 'He said you'd do this.

That you'd make up some crazy story about how he's trying to take over the country. You're so predictable.' She turns to Adanna. 'I bet you can't stand that you're no longer Dr Dòyìnbó's favourite and that it's finally my turn to shine.'

Adanna rolls her eyes. 'That's so stupid.'

'Is it?' Ẹni replies with a raise of her eyebrow. 'Did you ever stop to think about how I felt after you got your second Ike. After you ditched me.'

'I didn't—'

'Yes, you did,' Ẹni yells over her. 'All you cared about was your new power and Dr Dòyìnbó's attention that it was like I no longer existed. Well now I'm the one who has his attention.'

'Erm . . .' I begin. 'That's not as great as you think it is.'

Ẹni gives me a stinky look. 'Whatever. We're done with your stories.'

'It's not a story.' I look at Ọrẹ this time and spread my hands. 'We're trying to warn you.'

'Then why were you hacking into DAMI?' Ọrẹ replies, an unhappy expression on his face.

Okay, so when he puts it like that, breaking into the academy's artificial intelligence system doesn't sound good. I glance at Adanna quickly, but she says nothing. Before I can reply, Fọlákúnlé steps forward.

'Hacking into DAMI isn't very friendly behaviour.'

'And you couldn't even do that properly,' Ẹni taunts Adanna. 'Dr Dòyìnbó traced your hack. You led us straight here.'

Beside me, Adanna stiffens. *So that's how they found us . . .*

'None of that matters,' Niyì pipes up. 'Dr Dòyìnbó isn't who you think he is. He's a—'

'That's enough!' Ẹni shouts, cutting him off. 'We're not listening to any more of your stories. You're no longer Nchebe. We are!' Her voice ends on a triumphant note.

'Chai!' Hassan gasps, and Adanna sucks in a sharp breath.

Niyì says nothing, but the expression on his face speaks loudly enough.

I can't believe Dr Dòyìnbó has given Ẹni and her knock-off sidekicks the title of Nchebe. I know how much being Nchebe means to Niyì . . . to all three of them. This is just another way for Dr Dòyìnbó to hurt us. I know I'm right when I see the arrogant expression plastered across Ẹni's face.

'You're coming back with us,' she says. 'Dr Dòyìnbó gave us permission to do whatever it takes.'

I can tell Ẹni wants a fight, but our beef isn't with her. Dr Dòyìnbó is the real enemy, but I don't know how to convince her of that. Adanna was right. We can't go back to the academy yet.

'We no go follow you back,' Hassan replies, mirroring my thoughts.

Ẹni says nothing and instead nods at Ọ̀rẹ́ and Fọlákúnlé. They spread apart immediately, trying to circle us. Then Ẹni dives at Adanna, her body stretching in the air like an elastic band.

'Get Aunt Naomi to the Gyrfalcon,' I hiss at Niyì while keeping one eye on an advancing Fọlákúnlé.

He nods just as Òrẹ́ darts towards Hassan. I lose sight of Niyì as Fọlákúnlé begins to shake. The vibrations increase until suddenly there's two of him standing in front of me. I stare in shock at the perfect replica, right down to his clothes and the faint sheen of oil in his hair. My eyes flicker between the two versions, but neither moves.

Panic rushes through me. I'd heard about Fọlákúnlé and his dupes, but this is the first time I've seen it happen up close. I use the fear pushing through me to call up my Ike and I anchor it quickly. My hair whips up into a defensive arc around me.

'We don't have to do this,' I growl, narrowing my eyes at him.

The two Fọlákúnlés step forward. 'But we want to,' they say in perfect unison.

Suddenly, there are more of them – four, six, then eight. They multiply at a dizzying rate. I retreat backwards, but soon I'm surrounded, and I understand why Ẹni looked so smug. Fọlákúnlé is a whole army all by himself.

The world slows as they press into me from all sides, blocking my view of my friends. One of Fọlákúnlé's dupes swings towards me, and I strike out with a bolt of hair. He goes flying, but when he hits the ground, he disappears like a ghost. Another one lunges forward, and I flick him away too like an annoying fly. The same thing happens again, but the horde of Fọlákúnlés keep coming like they could do this all day.

'Find his weakness,' Adanna shouts.

My eyes sweep towards her voice. Ẹni's arm is wrapped around Adanna's upper body like a living hula hoop. Nearby, Òrẹ́ levitates through the air as he tries to dodge Hassan's energy shield. I can't see Nìyì or Aunt Naomi anywhere, so I can only hope they made it to the jet. Suddenly, Ẹni starts laughing hysterically, her stretchy body convulsing. It takes me a moment to realize that Adanna is tickling her, until she manages to free one arm, then the other.

'The dupes will disappear if you take out the original Fọlákúnlé,' Adanna adds, before pushing a still giggling Ẹni away.

Adanna's right. It's one of the first lessons Ms Bello taught us in self-defence class: figure out your opponent's weakness. Ẹni is ridiculously ticklish, while Òrẹ́ is impulsive. I turn my attention back to Fọlákúnlé's dupes advancing towards me. They're all controlled by the original version of him.

'Hey, Fọlákúnlé,' I call out, searching through them. 'Where you at?'

'We're not telling,' the horde of Fọlákúnlés chorus back at me, and I fight the urge to cover my ears.

The duplicates push forward, stalking me like hungry wolves. I shift, my hair rippling around me as they spread out in a wide semi-circle, each one ready to pounce at any moment. I move then, swinging my hair fast in a wide arc that punches through two of the dupes. They melt away on impact, but as they do, two more close in on me again.

Soon I'm spinning and weaving in an intricate dance of hair and fists as I try to fight them off. I don't see the leg that flashes out, tripping me up. My left foot skids out from under me and I go sprawling to the muddy ground, landing right on my bum. The laughter of the dupes above me fills my ears and the tangy smell of dirt blocks my nose.

They swarm me and I'm immediately lost under the press of restraining hands. I'm panting as they hold me down, making it difficult to use Ike. Then two of the dupes lift me by my arms until I'm upright and trapped on all sides, a multitude of hands in my hair. I look up at the sound of approaching feet. One of the Fọlákúnlés approaches with a look that promises pain written all over his face. I suck in a sharp breath, but then he pauses. My eyes drop to his neck, and something clicks. My gaze swivels quickly to the dupes on either side of me to confirm.

Not a single gold chain in sight.

My eyes move across the yard frantically searching. Then I find him. Standing apart from the others is a lone Fọlákúnlé. A strained look of concentration fills his face as he stares at me. I check his neck and see it. A flash of gold.

'Found you,' I yell at him.

He blinks in shock, and I feel the arms holding me weaken. I don't hesitate. A bolt of hair breaks free, whipping through the air. It hits him in the chest and he flies backwards onto the hard ground, landing in a confused heap.

The effect is immediate. The hands holding me disappear

and the remaining dupes surrounding me melt away one by one until there's only a single Fọlákúnlé left. Except now he's too busy running away to be a problem.

I exhale in relief, but it only lasts a moment as I search for my friends. I find Adanna standing over Ẹni, who's also on the ground, her stretchy body wrapped in on itself like an angry, muddy pretzel.

'How?' I ask her, disbelief and laughter tinging my voice.

'She talks too much,' Adanna replies with a satisfied grin.

'I no wan injure you,' Hassan shouts, his voice strained.

We both turn to find Ọ̀rẹ́ trapped inside one of Hassan's yellow energy fields. Just then, a mighty roar fills the air, and Ọ̀rẹ́'s eyes widen as the Gyrfalcon bursts through the massive, wooden barn doors. I stagger back as the sleek, black jet looms over us. It glides out of its hiding place, coming to a stop alongside us. The side doors slide apart, revealing a worried-looking Niyì.

'We have to go. There are more soldiers on the way.'

I turn back to Ọ̀rẹ́, unsure about what to do with him. But something in his face has changed.

'Drop the shield,' I tell Hassan.

He looks at me like I'm crazy but does it anyway. Adanna steps closer to Ọ̀rẹ́, who lifts an arm protectively. She waves it away impatiently.

'We're not lying,' she tells him. 'Why do you think using Ike makes Solari so sick?'

Ọ̀rẹ́ shakes his head, a pained expression on his face. 'I can't listen to this.'

'Fine,' Adanna says, then her expression turns pleading. 'The truth is in Scrabble.'

Ọ̀rẹ́'s eyes widen at Adanna's strange words, then he looks away, his face hardening. Adanna sighs and turns to the Gyrfalcon.

'Let's go. There's nothing left for us here.'

The jet is dead quiet. It's been about thirty minutes since we left the farmhouse, but no one has said anything. Adanna's been pacing for about fifteen of them, and Niyì and Hassan are huddled in their seats playing a game on their phones. Aunt Naomi still looks shattered from using her Ike, her body slumped in her seat.

'Did you hear what that nonsense girl said?' Adanna finally speaks up. '*We're Nchebe*,' she continues, mimicking Ẹni's whiny voice.

'Seriously?' Niyì mutters, looking up from his game. 'That's what you're worried about?'

'But she—' Adanna begins.

'We were totally ambushed back there,' Niyì yells, running a hand across his face. 'We've lost all of Auntie Naomi's research, and we've got nowhere to go, but, yeah, carry on worrying about losing a title.'

Adanna's mouth snaps shut, but only for a split second.

'We didn't lose all of it,' she replies quietly, before pulling something out of her back pocket. 'We've still got this.' She waves my father's digital pad in the air. Then she turns, moving to one of the storage compartments at the back of the jet. She pulls out two big black bags. 'And these.'

Hassan pounces on the bags immediately. 'Wetin be dis?'

Adanna shrugs. 'I stashed some emergency supplies in here in case we ever had to leave the farmhouse in a hurry.' She pulls a silver hard drive from one of the bags. 'I also backed up the data from the lab on these. It's a couple of days out of date, but most of it's there.'

'Ada, you do well o,' Hassan says as he pulls out a bag of snacks. 'You packed chin chin, sef.'

'What are we supposed to do with that hard drive?' Niyì says grudgingly.

Aunt Naomi straightens. 'The farm is just one of a network of houses I set up when I was on the run. There's another one not too far away. We can regroup there.'

Adanna frowns. 'Is the location stored in any of the computers at the farmhouse?'

Aunt Naomi's face drops. 'Erm . . . I . . .'

'I didn't have time to wipe all the computers,' Adanna says. 'Dr Dòyìnbó could find us again.' Then her expression turns thoughtful. 'We can't take that risk.'

'I know that look,' Niyì says. 'You've got a plan.'

Adanna comes to stand in front of him. 'We need to find the Rogues.'

Niyì flinches and a conflicted look stretches over his face.

Adanna touches his shoulder. 'I know you don't think it's a good idea, but we don't have a choice any more. We all want to take Dr Dòyìnbó down, but what happened at the farmhouse proves that we can't do it on our own. We need help.'

A silent stare-off begins between them until finally Niyì nods, then his head drops. Adanna moves past him until she's in front of Hassan and he gives her a thumbs-up. Her gaze flicks to Aunt Naomi, whose only answer is a small smile. Then Adanna is in front of me.

'Auntie Naomi and I can't figure out how to restore Niyì's Ike. We've tried, but we need your dad, and the Rogues are our best chance of finding him.'

Her words hit me in two places at once, and the cowrie shell hanging from my neck suddenly feels heavy. Adanna knows how much I want to get Niyì's Ike back. She also knows how badly I need to find my parents. I can't argue with her. *Just how long has she been planning that little speech?*

'Fine,' I finally whisper. 'Let's find the Rogues.'

CHAPTER SEVEN

Dark clouds fill the sky as I approach the creek's bank. Mangrove trees line the edge, but they look wrong. Gone is the thick, green canopy of leaves that used to blanket us. All that's left now are their twisted, gnarled roots rotting in the water. If you can even call it water any more.

The stream is dark and slick with the shiny brown glaze of crude oil. It coats everything, even the ground, and I hop over a bubbling puddle. I pass several boats, long abandoned by their owners, but my father's is missing. He must still be out fishing.

A sudden roar comes from somewhere in the distance, and a bright orange ball of flame shoots into the sky from a gas flare. My father says it's part of the process of extracting oil from the ground and we have to put up with it. My mother says it's polluting the rain and causing me to cough.

But these are not my thoughts, nor are they my memories. I'm someone else again. Something tickles the back of my brain – a faint reminder that I should guard my mind and build my shield. But I can't hold on to the thought and it slips away.

Then I spot my father's boat approaching the bank and, as it nears, he jumps into the water, pulling the boat to shore with him. Black sludge drips down his legs, turning his skin even darker.

'Did you catch anything?' I ask him when he reaches me.

Even the shake of his head is tired as he wipes his forehead. 'Nothing lives in these waters any more,' he says.

Nothing lives on the land either. At least that's what the local farmers say. Another roar from the gas flare echoes around us as it belches out its toxic fumes. Then, a thick, black plume of smoke billows into the air, merging with the already darkened clouds. As if they too have had enough, the clouds release their heavy burden and rain begins to pour down on us.

'We must get inside now.' My father's eyes dart about frantically, looking for shelter.

I know why he's worried. I can already feel the tightness in my throat and the cough bubbling up in my chest. It's always worse when it rains. The cough escapes in a hacking gasp and my father looks at me sharply.

'Do you have your inhaler?'

'Yes,' I wheeze, pulling it quickly from my pocket. But my hands are shaking too much, and the inhaler slips from my fingers. The light blue plastic hits the ground and is swallowed up almost immediately by a puddle of oily residue. My father drops down, scrambling in the dirt to find it. Then, after a thorough wipe on his shirt, it's back in my hand.

'Quickly,' my father says.

His voice is tight with fear, and I nod back because I don't think my own voice will work. I place the inhaler between my lips and push down hard on the pump. A puff of medicine rushes into my mouth, but my timing is off, and I barely take any in.

My father's hand covers mine and our eyes meet. 'Slow down and breathe deeply!'

With a desperate gasp, I suck in the thick vapour and fall into oblivion.

The darkness clears and the warm strength of my father's hand fades. In its place is the empty space again. I'm in a chair and opposite me sits a man, a familiar uniformed boy standing behind him.

Dr Dòyìnbó's lips lift in a confident smile. 'I told you we'd meet again.' My eyes flick to Tósìn and Dr Dòyìnbó's smile widens. 'He can't hear us. Tósìn is but a channel connecting our minds. Anytime you dream, he's able to find you.'

Horror fills me as his words sink in. Even in my dreams I'm being hunted.

'Why are you doing this?' My hands are shaking. The memory of my last gasp for air is still so fresh. 'Why are you showing me these visions?'

'So that you'll understand. Without me, that's what Nigeria would have become. And without me, that's what Nigeria will be once more.'

I shake my head. 'You don't know that.'

Dr Dòyìnbó gives me a pitying look. 'Don't I?'

'I don't believe you,' I snap. 'You're a liar, and you tried to take away my Ike.'

'That was a mistake – one which I now regret.' Dr Dòyìnbó leans in closer. 'We don't have to be enemies. You can help me protect our precious country.'

'We are!' I spit back at him. Dr Dòyìnbó rears back at the venom in my voice. 'You took away my family,' I continue. 'You hurt the people I love.'

Dr Dòyìnbó spins away abruptly. 'Do you think you're the only one who's had to sacrifice something? I, too, have known loss.' His head drops and he sighs deeply. 'For any great change to happen, there's always a price to pay, and I have paid it willingly.'

I blink at him, confused. But before I can ask what's he's on about, Dr Dòyìnbó whirls back round.

'You cannot stop me. You will not stop me!' Then his eyes blaze a promise at me. 'We are Solari, and soon the whole world will know what that means.'

Horrified by his words, I throw up my mental shield, repeating the word Nchebe over and over again. I should have done it as soon as I realized what was happening. Immediately, Dr Dòyìnbó fades away as my mind floats back to consciousness.

*

'Good, you're awake.' Adanna's voice is a loud welcome, and I open my eyes to find her beside me. 'We've arrived in Kano.'

I rub my face sleepily. 'Is the Gyrfalcon still in stealth mode?'

'Yes, but I've switched over from the solar batteries to eco fuel until we can recharge.'

'How long was I asleep?' I don't even remember closing my eyes.

'About an hour. What were you dreaming about?' Adanna asks with a frown. 'You smelled funny and your hair was floating.'

I'm about to tell her, but the gruffness in her voice stops me. Adanna will totally have a go at me for not protecting my mind better. Yet another mistake to add to my growing list. But there's something else stopping me too. I can hear the worry behind her harsh tone, and it reminds me of Mum. All the times she hid her fear behind anger and masked her concern with distance. It solidifies my decision. *I can handle this myself.*

'Why did you mention Scrabble when you were talking to Òrẹ́?' I ask instead, hoping to distract her.

It works and Adanna grimaces at me. 'Òrẹ́ and I used to play online Scrabble together before all of this happened. I usually won, though he was getting better at it.'

'Okay,' I reply, not really understanding her point.

Adanna rolls her eyes. 'I wasn't just hacking into AOSnet for fun, no matter what Niyì thinks. I left some clues for Òrẹ́ inside the game, in case we don't . . .' Her voice trails off and she shrugs. 'You know.'

I do, even though I don't want to think about it. Adanna's face is tight with unspoken pain, and I know immediately why. I place a hand on her shoulder.

'It's not your fault Dr Dòyìnbó found us.' I squeeze gently. 'He probably would have located us eventually, and it could just as easily have been Hassan's snoring that led him to us.'

Adanna's eyes widen, then we both burst into laughter. After a moment, Hassan comes to join us, and the quizzical look on his face makes us laugh even harder.

'Wetin be de matter?'

'Nothing,' I say, wiping a small tear from the corner of my eye.

Hassan shrugs, totally unbothered. 'We go make de call now?'

I look at Adanna and she shrugs.

'We were waiting for you to wake up before we called the Rogues.' She shakes her head like she can't believe what we're about to do. 'If we're going to do this, we need to do it together, especially if it's potentially a trap.'

I try not to think about that possibility as the three of us move to the front of the jet where Aunt Naomi is waiting. We don't have any other options left at this point.

'Bros?' Hassan calls to Niyì.

He doesn't even look up. 'I'm fine here.'

Adanna sighs, then dials the mysterious number on the Gyrfalcon's comms system. There's a steady beep, and just when I think the call's not going to connect, someone answers.

'Who is this, and where did you get this number?'

The voice is deep and rough, suspicion coating every word. Adanna nods at me to speak and I take a deep breath.

'My name is Onyeka Uduike, and I'd like to speak to Mr Gbénga, please.'

There's a long pause.

'You've got the wrong number.' The reply is short, sharp and dismissive.

'Wait!' I shout before the voice can disappear. 'My father is Benjamin Uduike. I know all about the sickness affecting the Solari.'

'Onyeka,' Adanna hisses, but I raise a hand to stop her.

I know the phoneline might not be secure, but this might be our only chance to get through to the Rogues and I'm not going to waste it.

'We know about Dr Dòyìnbó's true plans and we need to stop him,' I declare in a breathless rush.

There's another pause and my fingers clench into a fist by my side. Then the voice comes again, even sharper.

'Who's *we*?'

'Other Solari,' I reply. 'They want to defeat Dr Dòyìnbó too.'

'That's an interesting story, but even if I believed you, I can't help you.'

My fist tightens and my nails dig painfully into my palm. 'My father left me a message saying I should find you so that you could help us. Was he wrong?'

'I can't help you,' the voice repeats, and my heart sinks at the note of finality.

Then Adanna sighs. 'We have the thing you've been looking for.' Her voice is low and urgent.

The voice at the other end of the line exhales sharply. 'What did you say?'

'We have the serum,' I add quickly, sensing an opportunity.

Adanna pokes me hard, but I ignore her. A strange noise comes from the comms line that sounds like muffled voices having a discussion.

'This line is not secure,' the voice finally says, and Adanna throws me a look that screams, *I told you so*. 'In one hour, I'll send some co-ordinates on an encrypted line. Be ready.'

Then the line disconnects, and I breathe out a shaky breath. *We did it.*

'Na wa o,' Hassan exclaims, wiping his forehead, and I nod in agreement. That was proper intense.

Niyì finally joins us. 'So, what now?'

I shrug. 'We get ready.'

CHAPTER EIGHT

Just as the voice promised, a set of co-ordinates is sent through an encrypted message exactly an hour later with a location thirty kilometres outside of Kano. I track our progress on the Gyrfalcon's viewscreen, totally fascinated by the ancient city below us.

We pass several of the fifteen gates scattered across Kano – all that's left of the old city walls. The reddish-brown structures are now covered in a protective layer of solar glass. Just like in Lagos, many of the buildings use hydroponic farming to grow food. Vines and leaves spill down the sides of solar-panelled walls, covering them in colourful plant life like a second skin. There are parks and playgrounds filled with people living their everyday lives, while bright yellow electric tricycles carry passengers on their way. The mosques are something else too. Rounded domes made from more solar glass, flanked by skinny, gold-flecked minarets, shimmer under the fading glare of the sun.

'If you like wetin you dey see,' Hassan says, coming up beside me, 'make you wait to see am when Durbar festival dey happen.'

I frown at the unfamiliar word. 'Durbar?'

'It's an annual festival that marks the end of Eid el-Kabir,' Adanna says from her seat. 'Lots of colour, noise and horses. It's quite spectacular, actually.'

I can already imagine it. The city really is beautiful. Cheyenne would love it. I haven't been able to message her because I left my phone at the farmhouse, and Adanna won't let me call her from the Gyrfalcon. It's hard not being able to talk to her about what's going on. Cheyenne is my girl, and she's always the first person I go to when things get tricky.

We follow the looping motorways as they snake through the city. Hyperloop tracks criss-cross over them as the metallic pods speed along. A small hill rises out of the rich red earth and people clamber up the wide stairway winding up towards its flat peak. They look like scurrying ants from up here.

'Na Dala Hill be dat,' Hassan says, pointing to it. There's a thrum of excitement in his voice. 'Na where Kano begin be dat.'

As we push out of the city, the buildings grow fewer, and we pass a large solar tower power plant. Rows of mirrors are laid out in a circular pattern, and they glint at us in the last of the sunlight. From the air, it looks like a shimmery, reflective sun, carved into the rust-coloured soil. Rising from the centre is a single tower, beaming out a halo of light. Adanna says the mirrors are called heliostats, and they focus the sun's rays onto the tower to collect the energy.

It's getting dark by the time we land near the edge of a thick forest and leave the Gyrfalcon. About ten minutes later, a twin set of bright beams pierce the semi-darkness like glaring eyes. I blink. Whatever it is, it's heading straight for us.

The vehicle nears and I immediately spot that it's covered in solar panels, just like the Beast – the massive car we used back at the academy. But that's where the similarities end. While the Beast is all dark, hard edges, this car is pale grey, smooth and sleek like a dolphin. The front is solid with a jutting snout, and I reckon it could batter its way through anything. It comes to a stop, but the lights stay on, illuminating us like performers under a spotlight.

Then the side door swings open, and two figures climb out. Dressed in all black, the boy is short and stocky, and resting on his right shoulder is a vibrant yellow agama lizard. But it's the girl with a bright pink tapered Afro who has my attention. I know her, but I can't figure out where from. Then she turns bright red eyes on me, and I freeze. *I've definitely seen her before!* She broke into AOS after Ìdánwò and she attacked me and Niyì at the abandoned factories in Lagos.

'It's you,' I breathe, stepping backwards.

Her lips lift in a smirk, and behind her two more figures exit the vehicle. They form a protective guard as she and her companion move closer. Behind me, Nchebe and my aunt shift around me too, mirroring them.

'We haven't been introduced properly,' the girl says. 'My name's Zahrah, and this is Uche.'

The boy nods at me, and I swear his lizard does as well.

'That's Ada, Niyì, Hassan and my aunt Naomi,' I reply. 'I'm Onyeka.'

'I know.'

Of course she does. That must be why she's here – she can confirm who I am. *The Rogues really aren't taking any risks.* A part of me is glad, because that makes them smart allies, but it also makes them dangerous too.

'Nice haircut,' Niyì says in a tight voice, but Zahrah ignores him.

'We need to leave,' she announces. 'It's not safe being out in the open for very long.'

'You're kidding, right?' Niyì splutters. 'The last time we saw you, you tried to barbecue me, and now you want us to follow you, no questions asked?'

'Since you also tried to turn me into a block of ice, I think we're even,' Zahrah flashes back.

Niyì's mouth snaps shut, but his glare stays on full beam. I give him a warning look – *We're here to make friends, remember?*

'Where's Gbénga?' I ask carefully.

'At the compound,' Zahrah says and twists something on her

right thumb. 'I'll give the co-ordinates to your friends and the can meet us there.'

'Abeg o,' Hassan says sharply before I can reply. 'Who be us?'

Zahrah's left eyebrow lifts. 'Onyeka comes with us.'

'What?' Aunt Naomi gasps, as Niyì and Hassan shift closer to me.

'Not happening,' Adanna says at the same time.

I'm still processing Zahrah's demand when the short boy beside her finally speaks.

'If we're going to show you where we live, we need to make sure you aren't planning to do anything stupid with the information. Onyeka is our protection.'

Niyì snorts. 'She's a hostage, you mean?'

Zahrah shrugs. 'That's the deal. Take it or leave it.'

'We'll leave it, thanks,' Niyì replies. 'Come on, let's get out of here.'

He begins to turn away, Hassan and Aunt Naomi following him, but Adanna throws me a desperate look. I already know what she's thinking because I'm thinking it too. *We don't have a choice.* Besides, the Rogues need the serum, so they have no reason to hurt me.

'Wait,' I say. 'I'll come with you.'

Niyì spins round, disbelief stamped across his face. 'We can't split up.'

'Niyì's right,' Aunt Naomi says. 'I don't think this is a good idea.'

ly, and we'll be back together soon,' I reply way ... ntly than I actually feel. But the look of betrayal ... almost has me changing my mind.

Adanna nods at me and it gives me the courage to take a step forward. When no one else protests, I take another. Before I know it, I'm beside Zahrah. She looks at the friends I just walked away from, then her gaze returns to me. A strange mix of confusion and curiosity flitters across her face, then she lifts her hand again and begins tapping. I'm close enough this time to see the thick black cuff ring wrapped around her thumb and the small holographic screen above it.

'Here are the co-ordinates and a code,' Zahrah says, handing me a tiny memory drive. 'Your friends will need to transmit the code before they can land. It'll let our security system know that they're not a threat.'

She returns to the car, but Uche and the other Rogues remain, standing guard over me. The lizard on Uche's shoulder flicks its tiny tongue in my direction, as if it's taunting me.

'You sure say you wan stay?' Hassan asks, coming close and taking the memory drive from me.

I'm really not, but I nod anyway. Then I'm in Aunt Naomi's arms and she's squeezing me tight.

'We'll see you soon, okay?'

I nod again, because I don't think I can talk. If I try, I'll probably change my mind.

Adanna squeezes my arm. 'I promise I'll break all their heads if anything happens to you.'

Uche snorts at Adanna's fierce declaration, but I smile because I know she'd follow through with the threat. The expression on Hassan's face is a promise just as fierce as Adanna's, but Niyì says nothing. He won't even look at me. With a sigh, I turn to the car, Uche and the two others following me.

Inside, the vehicle is surprisingly simple, with two seats in front and an additional two rows of seats in the back facing each other. Uche moves into the driver's position, but there's no steering wheel, just a strange palm-sized console where a hand brake would normally be. Uche places his hand on it, and it lights up with a low pulsing sound. The pulse quickens as if it's tuning into Uche's heartbeat. Then the whole car comes alive and then we're moving.

Zahrah returns her attention to the device on her finger, making no attempt to talk, which is fine by me. I turn to look out of the tinted window as the landscape begins to change. The dense trees of the forest fade away, giving way to a grassy plain dotted with clumps of trees and street lights casting an eerie glow. We're so far out of Kano that the roads are completely deserted, except for a few carrybots. Their oversized heads sway as they glide along the pavement. The mobile street vending machines are popular in the northern provinces, and Adanna says they were designed to resemble street hawkers, who used to carry huge loads on their heads. It takes me a moment to clock

71

that the road isn't flat any more. We're climbing upwards, but towards what, I don't know.

Then a gravel driveway appears beneath a sign marked: DANGEROUS. KEEP OUT. We turn into it, and it's not long before we reach what appears to be a dead end. A solid wall of rock looms ahead. As we approach, a part of the rock face shimmers away as an entrance made of thick glass materializes. It looks like it's been carved into the wall.

The vehicle pulls up in front of it, and Zahrah gets out. I don't move. I'm frozen in place as the enormity of my decision finally hits me. *I'm on my own.* Zahrah looks through my window, her left eyebrow raised.

'Are you coming or not?'

CHAPTER
NINE

Zahrah's smirk is proper annoying, but I don't reply. Instead, I take a small breath, then step out of the car. As soon as I leave the vehicle, four more Rogues exit from the glass doors, also dressed in black. *Do these guys wear any other colours?*

'Where are we?' I ask.

'Our compound,' Zahrah says.

We move inside and I find myself in a stark white circular foyer. Artificial light pours down from the ceiling, illuminating the vibrant green walls and a huge sculpture in the centre of the space. Made from wooden vines, two thick interconnected strands wind upwards in the shape of a double helix ... *Our DNA.* It towers over everything like a guardian angel.

I'm so distracted by the sculpture that it takes me a moment to clock the strange texture of the walls. I squint hard, trying to get a better look. Then it hits me ... They're covered in a thick, dense moss. A steel gate stretches across one end of the room, with two fearsome-looking turnstiles protecting the way to whatever is on the other side. Beside them stands a Rogue guard, who discreetly glances our way. Zahrah ignores her, leading us to the first turnstile.

A second later, a soft blue light beams across her face and, after a short beep, scans it. I guess it liked her because the steel spikes part and she steps through. I get a glimpse of more metal doors before the barriers close again. Then it's my turn. The beam of light flashes and, to my surprise, the barriers open again. I step through to find a bank of lifts and Zahrah waiting impatiently by the nearest one.

Once Uche is through the security point, Zahrah uses the device round her finger to activate a security panel next to the lift, and the doors slide apart revealing a solid glass capsule. Zahrah and Uche step inside, and I follow slowly. As the doors close behind me, the capsule begins its descent. There's nothing to see at first but solid rock, then everything opens out suddenly as we hit the first underground floor and I freeze in shock. We're inside some kind of cavernous crater. Jagged grey walls of rock surround us on all sides, broken only by criss-crossing metal and glass-encased gangways that connect multiple structures in a complicated grid-like pattern. It's like I stepped into a scene from a spy movie.

The compound must have literally been built into the walls of the crater, and the only way seems to be down. Bright lights blaze from one glass-covered structure filled with row after row of plants, while thick pipes jut from another before feeding into the wall of the cavern. A thick cloud of steam swirls above it. My head bobs from left to right as I try to take it all in. Seeing my face, Zahrah smiles.

'It's an abandoned silver mine.' Her voice is thick with pride. 'There are four floors in total, all underground. This is the first level, which maintains the compound, and the lowest is the fourth.'

'Is there another way out?' I ask with a nervous glance at the walls surrounding us.

'Yes,' Zahrah replies, but she doesn't explain any further.

By the time the lift reaches the second floor, my ears are tight from the downward pressure. Before I can pop them, the metal doors spring apart to reveal a long corridor made of stone. The smooth grey walls are lit by a fluorescent strip of light embedded in the floor. Zahrah steps out and leads us down it past several rooms. There's an unnatural silence – a stillness almost. I thought it would smell bad underground, like Ogbunike Caves, but the air is fresh.

We finally stop at a set of double doors and Zahrah presses her cuff ring against a glass panel embedded in the wall. The doors slide apart silently to reveal a plush living space split into a lounge at the end closest to us and a dining area at the other.

A grey L-shaped sofa rests against the far wall of the

lounge, a large flat-screen TV hanging opposite. It looks like a mini apartment, but there's no warmth. Everything is perfectly placed and there's no clutter. There aren't even photos to suggest it's someone's home. There are more Rogues in this room. I count three kids my age and four adults in total. Straight-backed and alert, their eyes dart about, searching for danger. As one, they turn to look at us as we enter, and I finally notice the tall, moustached man sandwiched between them.

He's dressed in jeans and an orange-and-white buba top with a gold pattern embroidered on the collar and cuffs. On his head is a matching fila sat at a slight angle with the same gold embroidery running all the way round. He looks like a proud ọba, one of the old kings that used to rule the Yoruba people. Professor Sàlàkọ́ taught us about them during one of our history lessons back at the academy. My gaze moves to his unsmiling face to find a pair of deep-set eyes studying me with interest.

'Well, well, well. The lost daughter returns.' The man's voice is a gentle growl tinged with the musical inflections of his Nigerian accent. It *was* him on the phone. 'My name's Gbénga Akínmádé, but everyone calls me Ọ̀gá Gbénga,' he continues. He looks like a boss, so I'm not surprised that's how people refer to him. 'It's an honour to meet you, Onyeka.'

Now that I'm finally stood in front of Ọ̀gá Gbénga, I'm suddenly unsure what to do or say. All the questions I had

76

fly out of my head, and I stare at him like a muppet. I wish the others were here, I'm totally outnumbered. Aunt Naomi would have probably reached for my hand, and Hassan would have cracked a joke by now. Adanna would have definitely handled this better than me. There's no way she'd be silent.

'I've heard so much about you from Zahrah,' Ọ̀gá Gbénga says. 'Ike like yours must come with a unique set of challenges.'

'Yes,' I say, finally finding my voice. Then I picture Adanna and push back my shoulders to meet his gaze with more confidence than I feel. 'It also comes with a lot of tangles.'

Ọ̀gá Gbénga laughs, then turns to Zahrah. 'Were there any issues?'

She straightens immediately. 'No, sir. It went exactly to plan.'

'How long will it take the rest of the group to get here?' Ọ̀gá Gbénga asks.

Zahrah taps the cuff ring again and it flashes blue. 'They're already here. The jet arrived in the hangar ten minutes ago and they're on their way down now.' Relief fills me knowing that Nchebe and Aunt Naomi are nearby. 'Shall I collect them, Ọ̀gá?'

Ọ̀gá Gbénga nods, and Zahrah gives him a small salute before spinning round and striding away. Two of the adult Rogues break away to follow her as they return the way we entered.

'What do you think of my daughter?'

My mouth drops as my head swings back to Ọ̀gá Gbénga. *Rah! Zahrah is his daughter . . . And she calls him Ọ̀gá?*

'You don't look alike.'

I'm cringing before the words even fully leave my mouth. *What has that got to do with anything?* Luckily, Ọ̀gá Gbénga laughs.

'Well, you *do* look like Benjamin.' I flinch at the mention of my father. 'I'm sorry I wasn't able to save him.'

Save him? My heart flutters as I try to understand what Ọ̀gá Gbénga is saying. He can't mean what I think he means. *Can he?* My hands start to shake, and then it spreads until my whole body is practically vibrating from the emotion trying to break free.

Ọ̀gá Gbénga frowns at me. 'Onyeka? Are you all right?'

'W-when did he d-die?' I push out through trembling lips, as I fight to keep control of my Ike.

'Forgive me,' Ọ̀gá Gbénga says quickly, finally understanding. 'I didn't mean to scare you. Your father is very much alive.'

Alive . . . He's alive! I close my eyes as relief washes over me and my power recedes. *Thank you, God.*

'I've been looking for him since he disappeared,' Ọ̀gá Gbénga says quietly, and my eyes fly open again.

'You have?' I whisper.

Ọ̀gá Gbénga nods. 'Your father is our last hope. I believe I'm close—' His voice stops abruptly at the sound of approaching feet. I turn to see Nchebe and my aunt enter the room with Zahrah leading the way.

Adanna's eyes search my face as she reaches me. 'Are you okay? Do I need to break anybody's head?'

Ọgá Gbénga's left eyebrow lifts, and I shake my head quickly. 'I'm fine. This is Ọgá Gbénga.'

Aunt Naomi's eyes narrow. 'Ọgá?'

'It's just an honorary title,' Ọgá Gbénga says. 'It was given to me by my fellow Solari as a sign of respect.'

'Hello, I'm Adanna.' She steps forward and holds out her hand to Ọgá Gbénga. He takes it with a bemused smile. 'We've heard so much about you and the Rogues,' she continues, shaking it. 'Is it true that you have two Ike?' she adds eagerly. 'Do any of the other Rogues?'

Ọgá Gbénga's gaze sharpens, and beside him Zahrah's face tightens into a scowl.

'Rogues?' he asks with a quizzical look.

Hassan coughs in embarrassment, and Niyì throws Adanna a look of disbelief. But I understand Adanna's excitement. I know how desperate she's been to find Ọgá Gbénga. Back at the academy, the other students used to make fun of her because she has more than one Ike. It made her stand out, just like my hair did back in England. I know she's been desperate to meet another Solari like her – someone who understands what it's like to be different.

'Sorry,' Adanna says in a subdued voice, dropping Ọgá Gbénga's hand. 'It's what we . . . what Dr Dòyìnbó calls you.'

'We're not Rogues,' Zahrah spits. 'Dr Dòyìnbó is the rogue and so is everyone that's helped him.'

From the glare Zahrah's giving us, I reckon she thinks we were once those people.

'Dr Dòyìnbó lied to us,' Adanna snaps back with a glare of her own. 'That's why we're here. We want to make things right.'

Ọ̀gá Gbénga places a hand on Zahrah's shoulder. 'Peace, daughter.' Then he turns to Adanna. 'If you can't think of us as Solari, then you may call us Ọ̀mìnira. It means freedom, and it's what we've been fighting for.' Then he raises the hand on Zahrah's shoulder. 'And, yes, I have two gifts.'

Adanna's jaw drops as his whole arm begins to morph, the skin hardening as the light brown colour deepens into a luminescent black that shimmers under the lights. It almost looks like Mum's prized non-stick frying pan. My gaze swings to Ọ̀gá Gbénga's face, surprised by his casual use of Ike, but the strained expression reminds me of Aunt Naomi when she's using her Ike. Adanna doesn't appear to notice, and she takes a step closer, her scientific curiosity fully activated.

'Wow!' she breathes. 'Is that boron carbide? It's one of the hardest known materials in the world. It's why they call it black diamond.' Her hand reaches towards Ọ̀gá Gbénga's arm as if to touch it. 'What about your other Ike?'

Ọ̀gá Gbénga stiffens as her fingers draw closer, and his eyes shift to Zahrah. A strange look passes between them.

'That's something I don't discuss,' he replies in a voice as hard as his arm.

Adanna takes an uncertain step backwards, just as Niyì, Hassan and I move protectively around her. At the same time, Zahrah shifts closer to her father as his arm morphs back to normal. A tense silence fills the room.

What just happened?

CHAPTER TEN

'I-I'm sorry,' Adanna stammers as she pushes her Second Sight further up her nose. 'I wasn't . . . I didn't . . .'

Her voice trails off, leaving behind another awkward silence. Then Ọ̀gá Gbénga shakes his head.

'I'm sorry. That was no way to talk to a guest. We really are glad you're here.'

'Why?' Niyì replies, his voice full of suspicion.

Ọ̀gá Gbénga gives him a look of surprise. 'Your presence means that the truth about Dr Dòyìnbó is finally coming out.' Then his eyes zoom in on me. 'The serum means we once again have hope of curing this dreadful disease and reclaiming our Ike.'

A tight feeling stretches across the back of my neck. The eagerness in Ọ̀gá Gbénga's face makes me uncomfortable, and I can't help but wonder what the Òmìnira will do once they can use Ike freely.

'How did you find out about Dr Dòyìnbó?' Adanna asks carefully as her curiosity finds its confidence again. 'We've always been told that you left the academy because you were unhappy and wanted to destroy it, and that's why you kept attacking us.'

Ọ̀gá Gbénga's eyes widen. 'Nothing could be further from the truth. We were initially looking for Benjamin. Once I realized he wasn't at AOS, my focus shifted to finding new Solari before Dr Dòyìnbó could.'

'The attacks were a distraction,' Niyì breathes with dawning realization. 'Nchebe couldn't defend AOS and look for new Solari at the same time.'

Ọ̀gá Gbénga nods. 'Yes, though we weren't often successful. I believe there are still Solari out there waiting to be found.'

There's a pause as we all consider what this means. I'd always assumed that every new Solari made it to the academy, but what if there really are more out there? Alone and scared.

'How does Benjamin fit into any of this?' Aunt Naomi asks after a moment.

'He found me just before he disappeared. We hadn't even set up a proper base at that point,' Ọ̀gá Gbénga says, gesturing to the walls surrounding us. 'He told me he knew about Dr Dòyìnbó's true plans and he said he was working on a cure for the disease. In his final message, he said he'd finally cracked the serum, but there was a catch. Before I could find out any more, he was gone. Then you vanished, and soon after, Onyeka and her mother fled.'

Aunt Naomi nods. 'Benjamin made me promise to disappear if anything happened to him.'

'I worked that out eventually, but it was a huge blow. We'd finally found someone willing to testify to Dr Dòyìnbó's duplicity and a way to cure ourselves. Then we lost both overnight.'

Niyì narrows his eyes at Ọ̀gá Gbénga. 'How did *you* find out about Dr Dòyìnbó?'

'He told me himself.'

Aunt Naomi gasps, and Adanna throws me a look of confusion.

'Abeg, wait, I no get wetin you talk,' Hassan says, shaking his head.

Ọ̀gá Gbénga sighs. 'Dr Dòyìnbó never expected it to take this long to carry out his master plan. He's getting old and he's looking for a successor – someone he can trust to continue with his plans for Nigeria after he's gone. I was his first attempt at finding one. I was the perfect candidate too – top of my class and a member of Nchebe. I even saw Dr Dòyìnbó as a surrogate father figure. But I failed his final test. I wasn't willing to betray our fellow Solari to gain power.'

Niyì shifts from one foot to the other and I realize Dr Dòyìnbó was probably grooming him to be his next successor. I'm glad Niyì failed the test too.

'After Dr Dòyìnbó revealed his plans to me, I was horrified,' Ọ̀gá Gbénga continues. 'I knew I had to do something to stop him. I managed to convince a few of my closest friends, but no one else believed me. When Dr Dòyìnbó found out, he labelled us traitors and accused us of starting a revolt against him. We barely escaped the academy in time.'

'Why you no go meet Councils, make dem help you?' Hassan queries.

'I'd learned my lesson. If my own kind didn't believe me, why would anyone on the Councils trust my word? Once Dr Dòyìnbó's campaign of lies started, I knew we'd lost all hope.'

Adanna leans closer. 'So you've been living here ever since?'

'Not initially. The first few years were tough. We were constantly on the run and always watching our backs. As we found more Solari and grew in number, we realized we needed a permanent place to hide. Zahrah's mother found this mine and helped design the compound. She wanted us to have a place to call home. That's the kind of person she was.'

'Was?' Aunt Naomi asks.

Ọ̀gá Gbénga's face goes still, then he swallows like there's something stuck in his throat.

'She's no longer with us,' Zahrah answers in a low voice.

'Zahrah's mother valued Ike and the freedom to use it more than anything.' The expression on Ọ̀gá Gbénga's face reminds me of the one my mum wears when she thinks I'm not looking. A bitter sort of sadness.

'I'm so sorry,' I say quietly.

Ọ̀gá Gbénga glances down at me, a surprised look on his face.

Then his lips lift in a small smile. 'Second-generation Solari like Zahrah and yourself are so very rare. Not enough of us live to adulthood.'

'How many of you are there exactly?' Aunt Naomi asks.

Zahrah frowns at her like it's a big secret, but Ọ̀gá Gbénga merely shrugs.

'Just under two hundred,' he replies.

Aunt Naomi's eyes widen. 'Even with the sickness?'

'We try to limit the use of Ike. It's too dangerous for us adults. There aren't many grown Solari left. I know some of the original academy students, like you and Benjamin, have managed to survive the effects of the disease, but as far as we know, most, if not all, Protectors are dead. It's why Dr Dòyìnbó stepped up his plans. He's running out of Solari now that there are almost no new mutations.'

'This is our last chance to stop him, isn't it?' I ask as realization dawns.

Ọ̀gá Gbénga nods. 'I believe so.'

The room goes quiet again. We're all thinking the same thing. We're the last hope for Solari and Nigeria, maybe even the world. Dr Dòyìnbó won't stop with us. I've seen his visions; his fears. Everything he's done has been born out of some twisted need to protect the future. But if Dr Dòyìnbó succeeds, none of us here will have a future of our own. It's what my father was trying to prevent. It's the reason he risked his life.

'Dr Dòyìnbó has my mum too. Do you know where either

of my parents are?' I ask, trying to hold back the small spark of hope that's ready to ignite in my heart.

Ọ̀gá Gbénga shakes his head and my hope crashes back into the dark abyss of disappointment.

'But I believe I'm close to finding your father,' he says.

I suck in a sharp breath. 'What do you mean?'

'I embedded one of our own at the academy several years ago. It's how I knew about your arrival.'

I gape at him. *There's a Rogue spy at the academy?* My gaze shifts to my friends and they look as shocked as I feel. *Who is it?*

'Since your showdown, Dr Dòyìnbó has been very distracted. My spy is confident they'll soon have the information we seek,' Ọ̀gá Gbénga continues.

'Back up a minute,' Niyì says. 'You have a spy at AOS? Who?'

'I'm afraid I can't reveal that information at this point in time.'

'Why?' Niyì demands.

'It could compromise the mission. But come, we have more important things to discuss. You have the serum, yes?' he asks.

I nod, but an uneasy feeling niggles at the back of my mind. *Why won't he tell us who the spy is? What's he hiding from us?*

'Thank solar,' Ọ̀gá Gbénga says. 'We can finally cure ourselves and expose Dr Dòyìnbó for the fraud he is.'

'The serum—' Aunt Naomi begins.

'Isn't complete,' I cut in before I can even think about what I'm saying. An instinct I don't understand has taken over. 'The serum removes Ike,' I continue. The heat of Adanna's confused stare burns into me, but I don't dare look at her. 'It's the catch my father told you about before he disappeared.'

Ògá Gbénga's forehead scrunches up. 'I don't understand. I thought Benjamin was working on a serum to cure us.'

'He was, but my father wasn't able to perfect it in time,' I reply quickly, hoping desperately that no one gives me away. 'Niyì lost his powers when Dr Dòyìnbó used the serum on him. We've been working to find a way to reverse the effects of the current serum and create a new version that doesn't remove Ike.'

Ògá Gbénga's eyes narrow, examining me with an intensity that makes me want to squirm. 'You're saying the rest of you haven't taken the serum yet? That you still have the disease?'

The room is silent and a cold heat skates down my back. *Please back me up*, I plead silently.

'That's correct,' Aunt Naomi finally replies, and I almost sag in relief. 'I'm hopeful I can finish what my brother started, but we need time and a safe place to do so.'

There's silence once more as Ògá Gbénga absorbs everything. But something in my face must convince him because he suddenly sighs and his shoulders drop.

'That is disappointing news, but we can certainly provide both of those things. We have a fully resourced tech zone onsite and I'll make my best scientists available to you.'

'Thank you,' Aunt Naomi says with a small smile.

Ògá Gbénga nods, then abruptly looks down at a cuff ring

on his wedding finger with a distracted frown. It looks just like Zahrah's. A few seconds pass before his attention returns to us.

'If you'll forgive me, I have some other business to attend to. Zahrah will get you settled in one of the family quarters, and I look forward to seeing you at breakfast tomorrow.'

It's clear from his voice that we're done here, and Zahrah herds us towards the door. Just as we reach it, Ọ̀gá Gbénga's voice rings out loud and clear.

'Every resource at our disposal is now yours. Together we *will* defeat Dr Dòyìnbó. No matter what it takes.'

The family quarters are simple but pretty. The combined living area and kitchen is a big, open space bursting with colourful paintings. There's an oversized leather sofa, a dining table and chairs, and the back wall is made entirely of glass that looks out into the quarry beyond.

'Down the corridors,' Zahrah says, 'you'll find two twin bedrooms and a double. The bathrooms are stocked with all the usual toiletries, but let me know if you need anything else.'

'Where de food dey?' Hassan asks with a hopeful expression.

Zahrah points to the cupboards in the kitchen. 'Snacks are in there, and main meals are served in the dining hall on the third floor. Anything else?'

Aunt Naomi shakes her head, and as Zahrah turns to leave, Adanna steps in front of her, blocking her way.

'What's Ọgá Gbénga's second Ike?'

I frown at Adanna. That was blunt, even for her. I guess I didn't realize just how desperate she is to know.

'None of your business,' comes Zahrah's sharp reply.

'You said if we needed anything, we should ask,' Adanna pushes.

'I meant extra toiletries, not personal information.'

Zahrah moves, trying to sidestep Adanna, but she doesn't get far. Adanna's hand whips out, clamping down on her upper arm.

'Please. I need to know.' Adanna's eyes are pleading now. 'He's the first Solari I've ever met who's like me.'

Zahrah's eyes drop to Adanna's hand resting on her arm and her eyebrows lift. She's silent for so long that I start to wonder if she'll answer. Then she sighs.

'Fine, but if you tell anyone about this conversation, I'll deny I ever said anything,' Zahrah finally replies. 'He's an empath.' Adanna gasps, and Zahrah's mouth twists in response. 'But it's been a long time since he's let himself feel anything.'

With her strange words still hanging in the air, Zahrah turns and leaves. The door has barely closed behind her when Adanna rounds on me. Her hands are shaking.

'What was all that about?' she asks in a voice tight with suppressed anger.

'What?' I ask, trying to act innocent.

'Don't try that with me. You're rubbish at pretending.' I flinch, but she continues anyway. 'Why did you lie to Ọ̀gá Gbénga about the serum?'

I've been waiting for this. The whole way up to our quarters Adanna seethed silently in the corner of the lift. The others were quiet too.

'I don't think we should be revealing that information yet,' I finally reply with a small shrug.

Adanna's eyes narrow at me, and I try to think happy thoughts. She's like an emotional sniffer dog. Her eyes bore into mine, trying to smell out the truth.

'But they're Solari, and they want to help us,' Adanna replies finally.

'How do we know that?' I burst out. 'They could—'

I stop abruptly. *So much for keeping my emotions in check.*

'For solar's sake.' Adanna's hands lift, then drop helplessly. 'I can't talk to you.' She turns away. 'All I can hear is the roar of your fear.'

'I understand your concerns, Onyeka,' Aunt Naomi says, taking Adanna's place. 'But I don't think we should be keeping the cure from them. It's a dangerous precedent.'

'I don't want to keep it from them for ever. I just think we should wait until we're certain we can trust them.'

'I don't believe this,' Adanna mutters. 'They deserve to be cured too. This isn't what your father would've wanted.'

Something in me snaps at her casual mention of my father, and my Ike rises up in defence.

'Leave my father out of this,' I snarl as my thick braid whips out behind me. There's an awful silence as everyone watches me warily. I take a deep breath, trying to control the emotions raging through me. 'We'll tell them once we're sure Ọ̀gá Gbénga won't use it to create his own army,' I say, more softly this time.

Adanna's eyes narrow, watching me intently now.

'It's not like he fully trusts us either,' I rush on defensively. 'He wouldn't even tell us who his spy at AOS is.'

'This is about Dr Dòyìnbó, isn't it?' Adanna growls. 'I can smell the worry all over you.' Then her face evens out and her voice gentles. 'Not everyone is going to betray us, Onyeka.'

'I know that,' I mutter, even though I can't quite make myself believe it just yet.

'Do you?' Adanna replies, throwing me a knowing look.

'I'm with Onyeka on this one,' Niyì pipes up. 'I don't think we can afford to trust anyone too quickly.'

'Of course you don't,' Adanna snaps back. 'You see trouble everywhere.'

'That's because we keep ending up in trouble,' Niyì sneers. 'You're just trying to protect your precious Òmìnira.'

'And you're just a hippopotamus.'

'Look at your mouth,' Niyì replies with a snort. 'Can you even spell *hippopotamus*?'

Adanna doesn't even blink. 'N-I-Y-Ì.'

'Abeg!' Hassan shouts with a roll of his eyes. 'I dey tire of you two.'

'Whatever,' Niyì bursts out suddenly. 'You can ignore me, but don't say I didn't warn you.' Before any of us can stop him, he spins away. The doors part for him and he disappears through them.

Hassan sighs. 'Make I go talk to am.' Then he too is gone, leaving me, Adanna and Aunt Naomi staring at each other.

An annoyed sound leaves Adanna's mouth and the air almost crackles with her displeasure. 'I'm going to find the tech zone.' Without another word, she turns and stalks out of the room. The doors slide shut with an ominous softness behind her.

I close my eyes and take a deep breath. I don't understand what's happening to me. Why am I keeping secrets? First the dreams and now the serum. *Why can't I trust anyone these days?*

'That went well.' Aunt Naomi's dry voice cuts through my thoughts and I open my eyes.

'Do you think I made a mistake?' My voice isn't quite steady.

'I'm not sure, but I don't understand why you think Ọ̀gá Gbénga is lying to us.'

My parents lied to protect me. Dr Dòyìnbó lied to protect himself. Now I'm lying to protect my friends and family. We all have our reasons.

'I promise we won't have to lie for long,' I say out loud, though I'm not sure which one of us I'm trying to convince. 'It's just until we know we can one hundred per cent trust the Òmìnira.'

Aunt Naomi gives me hard stare, but her voice is gentle. 'Have you considered that you may never know?'

I swallow. I have no answer for her. All I know is that there's a knot in my belly. It's been there since we found out the truth about Dr Dòyìnbó, and I don't know how to loosen it. When I think about handing the serum over to Ọ̀gá Gbénga, the knot tightens, and a petrified voice screams in my head that it's too dangerous. I really want to trust the Òmìnira and to believe that we're finally safe, but something won't let me. Something inside me is broken and I don't know if it can ever be fixed.

CHAPTER
ELEVEN

What?!? Dr Dòyìnbó's people attacked u? U found the
Rogues? Where are u?

I sit up straighter on my bed as Cheyenne's message flashes
impatiently on the holographic screen projected over my palm.
It's coming from the new cuff ring wrapped round my middle
finger. I smile at Cheyenne's frantic reply. It's been over a week
since I last messaged her from the farmhouse – nine whole days
of keeping up a lie with the Òmìnira.

It took ages for Zahrah to approve our communicuffs, and
they only have the most basic functions and security clearance.
It turns out she's in charge of the compound's security, even
though she can't be more than two years older than me. I don't
think she trusts us any more than I trust her.

I glance back at my palm, and my finger moves quickly over the holographic keyboard as I type a reply.

Actually, they're called Òmìnira, and I can't tell u where we are. We're safe though, I swear.

Fine, keep ur secrets ...

I flinch at Cheyenne's reply. *She has no idea just how many secrets I'm keeping.* Then she leaves me on read for so long that I begin to worry she's genuinely angry at me. I try a different tactic.

Are u excited about camp?

A minute passes and still no reply.

Chey?

... I'm worried about u guys

The relieved breath that leaves me turns into a deep sigh. I'm worried about us too. Adanna's barely talking to me, and Niyì's even more distant than usual. The only person who seems anything like their regular self is Hassan. But he's been spending a lot of time with some of the younger Òmìnira, so I haven't seen much of him. Aunt Naomi's been in the tech zone night and day to try to find a way to restore Niyì's powers, all while pretending to be working on a serum that's already fixed. And we've barely used Ike in case someone realizes we're no longer sick.

It's only a matter of time until all my secrets catch up with me, but the only good thing is that I haven't had any more dreams. I don't like the person I'm turning into, but I don't know how to stop it. The screen flashes again.

U still there?

I can't tell Cheyenne any of this.

It's all good. By the time u get back from camp, we'll have everything sorted

Promise?

I hesitate. But what's one more lie at this point? I cross my fingers behind my back, though it's not like Cheyenne can see me.

Promise! Gotta go now. Speak soon

I don't wait for the reply and the projection fades until all I'm staring at are the brown lines criss-crossing my palm. My hand is shaking, and Ike rises up like a wave. It feeds hungrily on the guilt boiling in my body, and the thick braid hanging behind me begins to lift. I've stopped styling my hair into the usual loose bantu knots and the braid unravels before I can stop it. My hair fans out into a thick cloud of curls and coils and it tightens into a protective cocoon around me. I let it for a brief moment before I anchor my emotions and my hair drops back down instantly.

I look over to Adanna's bed, but it's empty as usual. If she's not in the tech zone with Aunt Naomi, she's usually off exploring the rest of the compound. I clench my trembling hand into a tight fist and close my eyes. *You can do this, Onyeka!*

I get myself ready for breakfast before I go looking for the one person who still feels familiar. As expected, I find Hassan in a prayer room inside the faith zone with a bunch of younger kids clustered around him, as if he's some kind of game they can't wait to play. Most of them are Solari that Ọgá Gbénga and the Òmìnira rescued, but a couple were actually born here at the compound. Hassan finally spots me and waves just as a little boy wearing a red T-shirt taps his leg.

'I want to come when you take down that doctor man,' says the little boy. 'I'm ready to fight.'

'Why are you so eager to fight?' Hassan replies. He doesn't use Pidgin with the younger kids as most of them don't understand it.

'He's a bad man, and we have to protect each other,' the same boy says. Then a look of uncertainty comes over his face. 'Don't we?'

Hassan nods. 'Yes, we should be ready to defend ourselves and the people we love, but that doesn't mean we should go looking for trouble.'

'Then how do we prove we're brave like you?' another boy asks.

Hassan smiles. 'Sometimes it's braver not to fight. The right words can be just as powerful as a punch.'

'I have lots of words,' a little girl with big eyes and a headscarf says confidently. 'When I'm bigger and I get my powers, I'll make sure everyone hears them!'

Hassan laughs then tickles her chubby cheeks until she starts giggling.

'I'm sure you will, Fatima,' he tells her.

Another boy raises his hand. 'What if we mess up when we use our Ike?'

Hassan's eyes narrow at the boy. 'What did you do, Ibrahim?'

'I might have teleported into the kitchen,' the boy replies with a guilty look. Hassan stays quiet, waiting for him to finish. 'I took some suya from the grill.'

Hassan looks at Ibrahim until he begins to fidget restlessly. 'I used to turn invisible to escape my classes,' he finally says in a gentle voice.

Ibrahim's eyes widen. 'Na wa o!'

Hassan laughs at the boy's attempt at Pidgin. I guess the kids have been watching him more closely than any of us realized.

'Don't tell Ọ̀gá I said that,' Hassan says. 'I've got to go now.'

The children all groan as he scrambles up and makes his way over to me.

'I'll see you later,' Hassan adds with a smile as we leave the room.

'You're really good with them,' I tell him as we make our way back down the corridor towards our quarters to collect Niyì.

Hassan shrugs. 'They remind me of home.' Then he switches back to Pidgin with a grimace. 'Small, small.'

'You must miss your family a lot,' I say softly.

'No be lie, e no easy. I dey miss my family well, well. I enter de academy because I wan help my country. Now every ting na lie, it pain me because I don waste my time for de academy.'

'Don't say that,' I plead. 'We're going to make everything right. Ọ̀gá Gbénga will help us.'

Hassan gives me the side-eye. 'Na now you dey trust am?'

'I don't know. Do you?' I stare at him curiously.

I know Adanna does, and Niyì thinks we shouldn't, but Hassan hasn't said much, which is proper weird for him. I think he's been distracted by being back in his home city and so close to his family. There's a new longing in his face that I recognize. If he could visit his parents, I know he would. The same way I'd give anything to find my mum and father.

Hassan shrugs again. 'Ọ̀gá Gbénga, e dey okay. But de wahala be de lying.'

He stops and gives me a knowing look. He's right, and deep down I know it. My lie is the problem. I look away and we continue walking. Soon we reach our quarters and Hassan uses his communicuff to activate the lock.

'Bros! You're late and I'm hungry.'

Niyì's irritated voice comes from somewhere inside their bedroom, and Hassan throws me an amused look before going in. I follow more slowly. Their room looks just like mine and Adanna's, except for the mess of stuff on Hassan's side. There's no way Adanna would let me get away with that.

I spy Niyì lounging on his bed. He looks like he hasn't left it in days. He might not have, to be fair. He spends most of his time in his room, only really coming out to eat or to argue with Adanna.

'What's going on?' he says once he spots me behind Hassan.

'We go chop. Hunger dey tear my bele o.'

'In here?' Niyì asks hopefully.

I shake my head. 'The dining hall.'

Niyì frowns. He hates eating in there with all the Òmìnira. I think it reminds him of the canteen back at the academy. With so many Solari in one room, the air is always charged with power. Hassan and Adanna love it, but I can't lie, I'm never entirely comfortable.

'Oya,' Hassan says. 'Dey go make Hausa Koko. We go chop well, well.'

Niyì tilts his head as he considers Hassan's offer. Hassan has been going on about how amazing the porridge made from millet is, especially with akara.

'Fine,' Niyì says, bolting upright. 'But it better be good.'

We head for the lifts that take us from the second underground level down to the third. While our floor is mostly living quarters, all the main activities happen down here. From the twenty-four-hour dining room, to the gym, where Zahrah and Uche run daily training sessions, and the cinema room, where they host popular movie nights.

The Òmìnira are like little worker ants, moving between tasks with a restless air that lingers at the compound. They're constantly alert, waiting for something to happen. But they know how to have fun too. There's always a party or happy gathering happening. There are no houses here. No tournaments or any kind of separation based on Ike. The Òmìnira are a family, and everyone works together. We're the outsiders looking in.

The dining room is mostly empty when we enter. It's late morning and most of the Òmìnira are back at their various jobs. From tending the crops and seafood in the hydroponic and fish farms on the first floor, to maintenance of the ground water pumps and geothermal plant that generates energy here. There's also security and teaching in the small school that all the Òmìnira children attend – it takes a lot of manpower to keep the compound running.

I spot Adanna at a table, but she's not alone. A noisy cluster of Òmìnira kids are there too, with Zahrah and Uche at the centre. So is the lizard that seems to live permanently on Uche's shoulder. I swear I saw its eyes flash yellow once. I told Aunt Naomi and she shrugged. She said there were rumours that the trarium contamination affected more than just us humans.

As we approach, it becomes clear what all the noise is about. Hovering in the air above the table are two holographic pen-like objects – one black and the other green. A circular ring of energy surrounds them both, beamed into the air by the holographic projectors embedded in the ceiling. Suddenly, Uche flicks the black pen in front of him and it slams into the green one. He whoops loudly as the green pen goes flying through the ring of energy before shattering into a kaleidoscope of fragmented light.

'That's three knock outs, Gbémisọ́lá. I win,' Uche shouts, and the tall girl beside him mutters something under her breath before sitting back down. 'Who am I beating next?' No one volunteers and Uche snorts his disappointment. Then his gaze lands on us. 'How about one of you?'

All heads turn in our direction and Adanna's eyes light up when she spies Hassan. They dim a little when she clocks me and Niyì right behind him. I say hi when we reach the group and I'm greeted loudly. Zahrah doesn't reply. Her attention stays fixed on the food in front of her. Her cropped hair is bright blue today. She's always changing the colour.

'Abeg wait. I dey come. Make I chop first,' Hassan says to Uche with a smile.

Uche grins back. 'Ehen. Maybe I'll have some proper competition now.'

There are groans from the Òmìnira surrounding us, but Uche is unbothered as he reaches for the agbalumo on this tray. He quickly bites off the top of the fruit before putting it into his mouth and sucking hard. The yellow flesh shrinks as he hoovers up the sweet-sour juice inside. Then he spits several dark seeds onto his plate. *Maybe that's his Ike.*

'Adanna was telling us all about the academy, and your dance battles,' Uche says with a small smirk as he tosses the shrivelled fruit aside. His lizard smirks back too. 'Sounds like a fun place.'

'It can be,' I reply carefully. The List and Idanwo aren't very fun. 'It seems more like a prison now that we know the truth.'

'That sounds familiar, eh, Zah?' Uche says giving Zahrah a nudge.

Heads swivel her way, but again she says nothing.

'The academy is still our home,' Niyì replies in a tight voice, and the heads ping pong back.

Uche spreads his arms out. 'This compound is our home too. That doesn't mean we like being trapped here, hiding from your head teacher.'

There's a new tension in the air, and the Òmìnira kids watch us now like excited spectators at a tennis match.

'Our fight is with Dr Dòyìnbó,' Adanna says slowly, trying to diffuse things. 'Not each other.'

Niyì bristles immediately. 'At least they know the truth about him here. The Solari at the academy are still in the dark and in danger.'

'We've been trying to warn you about Dr Dòyìnbó for years,' Uche flares back. 'So excuse me if I don't feel sorry for your pampered friends at your precious academy. We have our own problems too.'

Adanna winces and Niyì's eyes narrow dangerously, but before I can say anything, Zahrah finally speaks.

'We're not allowed to use Ike past the age of twenty. Every child here knows that becoming an adult means losing the very thing that makes us who we are.'

Is that why she's had such a stinky attitude with us? I remember how I felt when we first discovered the truth about the sickness, and I can't imagine feeling that way my whole life. In a twisted sort of way, the Solari at the academy are lucky to still be clueless about it.

'I'm sorry,' I say softly.

'Your apology won't cure us, will it?'

I flinch at the harshness in Zahrah's voice and quickly swallow the angry reply that's desperate to escape. I'm hiding the very thing that *could* cure them, and I have no defence. That doesn't stop Adanna trying though.

'Neither will your attitude,' she flashes back, even though I can tell she's still not happy with me.

'Have you told him that?' Uche says, nodding at Niyì. 'Or is he normally so useless?'

I wince as Niyì flinches.

'What's your problem?' he demands. 'You don't even know me.'

'My friend, look at your life,' Uche throws back. 'I've seen enough to tell me everything I need to know. You've done nothing but hide in your room since you got here.' He points at Niyì. 'Is that how you plan to take down your crazy head teacher?'

There are loud gasps from our audience, and Niyì looks at Hassan in disbelief. 'Is this bobo serious right now?'

Hassan shrugs, a helpless look on his face.

'This isn't getting us anywhere,' Adanna says, trying to calm things down again. 'We have to work together.'

'Like you lot?' Uche scoffs. 'Abeg, don't make me laugh! All you've done since you got here is eat and argue. No wonder Dr Dòyìnbó showed you pepper.'

Niyì steps closer so he's up in Uche's face, and the lizard on Uche's shoulder bristles in warning.

'*We* found the serum,' he spits out. '*We* stopped Dr Dòyìnbó from getting his hands on it, and *we* figured out—'

'How to find you,' I cut in quickly before Niyì can blab the truth. Now definitely isn't the right time.

'Well done,' Uche sneers, his eyes flashing. 'Do you want a medal or something?'

Zahrah stands suddenly and places a hand on Uche's shoulder. 'That's enough. We have training soon. Let's get out of here.'

Uche stiffens at the order in her voice and, in that moment, I understand why Zahrah's in charge of security. I thought it was because of her father, but the calm strength radiating from her is so powerful that it demands attention. Even Uche with his big chat is helpless to resist, and he shuts up. Then, without another word, the two of them leave the table and the dining room. The remaining Òmìnira follow silently.

I stare after them, my jaw clenched. I don't understand what Uche's deal is, and Zahrah's not much friendlier either. They act like we're working with Dr Dòyìnbó, but he lied to us too.

'What was that?' Niyì splutters.

Adanna ignores him and turns to me. 'I knew this lie was going to cause wahala,' she whispers in a harsh voice. 'It's not right.'

With those devastating words, she turns and leaves herself. I swallow hard. Adanna is right. My lie *is* causing a whole heap of trouble. There's a strained silence, and I don't know where to look, never mind what to say. Then Hassan points to the kitchen with an awkward cough.

'I dey go chop o. You wan come?'

I shake my head. I don't think I could eat now even if I wanted to.

CHAPTER
TWELVE

The corridors are quiet, the faint hum of the ventilation system the only thing keeping me company as I make my way to the tech zone. A little shiver of worry slides down my back. It's been there since I got the message to meet Adanna and my aunt. Adanna and I haven't spoken since what happened in the dining hall earlier this morning and a part of me is dreading seeing her.

The tech zone is located on the third floor too, just above the garage on the fourth level where the electric vehicles are kept. The Òmìnira use them when they venture out of the compound, and many can be operated remotely. The tech zone isn't as big as my father's lab in Lagos, but it has way more equipment. Double the size of our quarters, all the pretty furnishings have been stripped away, and instead they've been replaced by stark white walls and grey metal tables packed full of machinery and scientific apparatus. When I arrive, Adanna is at one of the computers, fiddling with the holomorpher from Aunt Naomi's farmhouse. *I still don't know what it does.* The Òmìnira scientists who usually work in the tech zone are missing, leaving just Adanna and my aunt.

'We need to talk,' Aunt Naomi says as soon as I sit down.

'What's wrong?' I ask. 'Have you found a way to get Niyì's Ike back?'

Aunt Naomi's eyes flick to Adanna and a look passes between the two of them. When Adanna turns back to the device on the table, I know it's not good news.

'I'm sorry, Onyeka, but we can't figure it out,' Aunt Naomi replies softly.

'But you said—'

Aunt Naomi lifts a hand that silences me. 'I said I'd do my best, but we've hit a dead end. Without your father, I don't know how to get past it. There's a vital piece of data I need, and we can't find it on the digital pad.'

'I thought Ada was sorting that out?'

Adanna swings back round. 'I tried,' she snaps. 'But I'm only Solari, not God.'

Aunt Naomi places a gentle hand on my shoulder. 'We need to find Benjamin. Has Ògá Gbénga said anything new about the search?'

'The last I heard, he was close,' I reply slowly, and Aunt Naomi frowns. 'I'll ask him again,' I add.

Aunt Naomi nods and begins to turn away.

'I think it's time to tell Ọ̀gá Gbénga about the new serum,' I blurt out.

'About time,' Adanna mutters, and my shoulders dip at her tone.

'It would certainly make things easier,' Aunt Naomi says, her stare turning intense. 'Do you want me to come with you?'

I shake my head. This is my mistake and it's up to me to fix it.

The Òmìnira that guard Ọ̀gá Gbénga's quarters never change. Emem is the friendliest of the two. She always gives me a smile, and some days she evens says hi back. Bukola is proper grumpy though. He reminds me of how Adanna used to be before we became friends. I swear the frown on Bukola's face is permanent, almost as though it moved in one day and has refused to leave since.

Today is no different. Emem gives me a small wave, while Bukola scowls before stepping aside. The doors slide apart and I enter. Even though I've been here before, the cold perfection of it still doesn't sit right with me. I find Ọ̀gá Gbénga and Zahrah in his office, bent over the massive desk that dominates the room. His fila is purple today.

Ọ̀gá Gbénga turns to Zahrah. 'Where are we with the defensive plan?'

'We're still only at ninety per cent efficiency,' she replies. 'So I've increased the training drills for everyone.'

'Iyen da,' *That's good*, he says with a nod. 'We need to be ready, just in case.' Ọ̀gá Gbénga looks up as I approach. 'Good afternoon, Onyeka. How can I help you today?'

Zahrah just stares at me, her red eyes blank and unreadable.

'Do you have an update on my parents?' I blurt out.

Ọ̀gá Gbénga's eyes widen at my abrupt question, then he shakes his head. 'Not yet, but these things take time. Dr Dòyìnbó is definitely distracted and he's bound to become careless. I believe we'll have a breakthrough soon.'

I frown. 'If he's distracted, shouldn't we make a move now? We need to tell everyone what he's been doing to the Solari at the academy.'

'We can't help anyone at the academy until we help ourselves first,' Ọ̀gá Gbénga replies. 'Once your aunt fixes the serum and we can cure ourselves, then we'll move.'

I swallow hard, my finger wrapping round a stray curl. This is my moment to end the lie.

'There's something I need to tell you,' I begin, but my voice breaks off abruptly as fear floods me. Ọ̀gá Gbénga is going to be so angry. *What if he decides not to help us because of my lie? I'll never find my parents or be able to save the Solari at AOS!*

'Is everything okay?' Ọ̀gá Gbénga asks, his narrowed eyes studying me.

My mind races frantically. *Does he suspect me already?* I swallow again, trying to decide what to do. The silence stretches and sweat breaks out across my nose despite the cool air rushing out of the vents above us. Zahrah stares at me strangely. Then Ọ̀gá Gbénga sighs softly.

'I'm supposed to meet your aunt in the tech zone for an update.'

I look away as the fiery itch of guilt burns across my skin. I need to get out of here . . . *now*!

'I just came from there,' I say, backing away quickly. 'They're still working on it.'

Zahrah's eyes narrow at me suspiciously, but Ọ̀gá Gbénga just looks concerned. I can't decide which is worse, so I turn and make my escape with a hurried goodbye.

I spend the rest of the day hiding in my bedroom, only surfacing to grab food. Now I understand why Niyì does it so much. By the time evening comes, I have a headache from all the worrying I've been doing. The cool sheets of my bed are such a relief and the pillow beneath my head so soft and welcoming that I don't even bother to wrap my hair with a silk scarf. It doesn't take long before my eyes begin to drift shut.

At some point in the night, I feel the pull of a dream. There's a moment, a split second, where I know I should fight it by protecting my mind from the invasion, but I'm so tired. Tired of fighting, of being scared all the time, of pretending to be strong. The truth is, I'm completely lost and only one person has the answers I'm desperate for.

I'm in a boat as it weaves through a strange assortment of shacks that rise up on skinny wooden legs resting in water so dark and murky you can barely see into it. Rubbish and sewage clog the waterways, drifting past like grim flotsam. Smoke swirls from many of the makeshift windows, filling my nose until I can hardly breathe. It's thick with the smell of fish and I want to gag, but I can't because I'm not alone.

'Welcome back,' my companion says without surprise.

I turn to face Dr Dòyìnbó. A kind smile lights up his face, almost as if he knows I'm too weak to fight any more. Tósìn is there too, an ever-silent presence connecting our minds.

'Where are we?' I ask.

'A place called Makoko, if I'd allowed it to exist,' Dr Dòyìnbó replies. 'It's a slum that floated off the coast of the mainland.'

Another one of his visions then, likely designed to convince me that his future is the only way. Even though it isn't real, I never imagined people could live like this. A woman passes us, her canoe bobbing gently in the water as she tries to sell her goods to the people in nearby boats. Her face is lined with age and struggle, but there's also determined hope there. I see it too on the smiling faces of the children around us as they clamber across the wooden verandas and swim between the rotting stilts on which their houses are built. This is their home. I recognize the expression because I used to see it on my mum's face every day when we were struggling to survive back in London.

'Where are my parents?' I ask in a flat voice. I'm done playing games.

Dr Dòyìnbó's smile turns sad. 'You know I can't tell you.'

I close my eyes. Of course he won't. What was I thinking letting him into my dreams again?

'I'm not playing any more,' I whisper harshly. It takes a second to call up the word that will end this awful dream. Nchebe. I let it form in my mind.

'Wait!' Dr Dòyìnbó's voice is urgent. 'What if you could end this? What if you could save your parents and friends?'

My eyes fly open at this unexpected offer. Even though I know I should shut the dream down right now, the lure of his words is too strong to ignore.

'What do you want?'

Dr Dòyìnbó pauses and his head tilts. 'You.'

'I don't understand,' I reply with a frown.

'I'll let your parents go, and even pardon your friends. All you have to do is help me ... Help me secure my legacy.'

'No!' I gasp, horrified.

'There's a link between us now,' Dr Dòyìnbó continues, as if I'd never spoken. His eyes flick to Tósìn. 'He's just discovered it and we don't know how it happened. Perhaps it's because you're the only second-generation Solari at AOS. I can't communicate directly in this way with any of my other students,' Dr Dòyìnbó says. 'I don't believe it's a coincidence that the universe has sent me a replacement – you, the child of my greatest student.'

His terrible words spin in my head and I try to make sense of them. A link? A replacement?

'I won't do it,' I finally growl. I can't, not even to save my parents. 'I won't help you.'

Dr Dòyìnbó's smile is back, but now he looks satisfied. 'You will. I told you, we're connected now, and I will find you.'

The smell of smoke begins to empty from my nose, and the water around us starts to fade.

'No! Wait. What do you mean?' I scramble forward, desperate. 'Tell me!' I scream, just as the canoe stills and the water melts away completely.

Dr Dòyìnbó's awful smile is the last thing I see before he too disappears.

What have I done?

Then a familiar voice calls out to me as if from a distance.

'Wake up, Yeka!'

CHAPTER THIRTEEN

Warm air from Adanna's mouth hits my ear and I shoot upright.

'Huh? Wh-what's going on?' I gasp.

'Calm down, it's just me.'

I rub my sleepy eyes with the back of my hand. 'What time is it?'

'It's six thirty in the morning,' Adanna says, and I groan. 'I know, but I need to take the Gyrfalcon out.'

'Why?' I ask confused.

Adanna shrugs. 'We need to charge the solar batteries so that they don't degrade, and we're less likely to be seen at this time.'

I sigh. 'Okay, I'll get ready.'

Her hand on my shoulder stops me. 'You're staying here Ọ̀gá Gbénga has asked to see you in an hour. He has something he wants to talk to you about. Besides, I'll only be gone a couple of hours.'

'What about the others?'

Adanna's face drops. 'They're coming with me, actually.'

'What?'

'Niyì insisted. I think he's fed up with being cooped up in here. I don't think Auntie Naomi likes it underground much either, and Hassan's coming to stop any arguments.'

I nod. Even with all the UV lights, it's been hard not seeing the sun. I also understand why Niyì wants to bolt. He's been even more moody since his run-in with Uche yesterday. When I don't say anything more, Adanna takes that as her sign to go, leaving me with only my thoughts for company.

I rub a hand across my face as the memory of my dream returns, taunting me. I should have put up my mental defences immediately.

There's a link between us now.

I knew there was something wrong about my dreams. Dr Dòyìnbó's final words come back to me – *I will find you* – and I remember the certainty in his smile. What if I've put us at risk? What if Dr Dòyìnbó figures out where we are through our link? It's time to tell Ọ̀gá Gbénga the truth about the serum, no matter how hard it might be.

I check my communicuff and realize I need to get a move on. I pull on a pair of shorts and a T-shirt and tie my hair up into bantu knots using Ike. The corridors are quiet as it's still early and I quickly grab breakfast before making my way to Ọ̀gá Gbénga's quarters.

I find him at the dining table in a high-backed chair, his face hidden by the news tablet in his hands. A half-eaten plate of yam and egg rests on the table in front of him. I cough loudly to let him know I'm there. The tablet lowers revealing Ògá Gbénga's face, and there's an expression of barely suppressed excitement stamped across it.

'Onyeka, there you are!' He gestures to the chair beside him, and I make my way over.

'Where's Zahrah?' I ask slowly.

'Her car was recently serviced, so she's gone to check it was completed properly.'

I nod. That sounds about right. Zahrah is a total perfectionist. Even during the training drills, she's never happy until everything is exactly the way she wants it.

'I have something to tell you,' I say, ready to come clean.

'Me first,' Ògá Gbénga says with a smile. 'I have some news about your father.'

His words drop like a grenade, blowing every other thought out of my mind. I lean forward excitedly. 'You found him?'

Ògá Gbénga's smile grows even wider and a warm hand covers mine. 'Yes. My spy at the academy was finally able to confirm a location. Dr Dòyìnbó has been keeping Benjamin in—'

But Ògá Gbénga doesn't finish as his voice fades away when the room and everything else in it starts shaking. The contents of the table go crashing to the floor and I drop down after them instinctively. Ògá Gbénga is right beside me, a look of shock on his face.

'What's going on?' I gasp.

But Ọ̀gá Gbénga isn't listening. He's too busy frantically tapping on his communicuff as the shaking continues around us. The ceiling above rumbles ominously and panic rises in me. I grab the leg of the table to steady myself just as a message finally comes back on Ọ̀gá Gbénga's cuff. His face tightens.

'There was an explosion on the ground floor,' he mutters. 'We're under attack.'

'From who?' I cry.

Ọ̀gá Gbénga grimaces. 'I have my guesses. We must have gotten careless.'

I stare back at him in horror. Could it be Dr Dòyìnbó? *Is this my fault?* A tight feeling settles in my chest. I knew I should never have let that dream continue. What if I've led Dr Dòyìnbó right to us?

'We need to get out of here,' Ọ̀gá Gbénga continues.

He stands and helps me out from under the dining table. Keeping a hold of my hand, he practically drags me to the doors of his quarters and out into the hallway, where his guards stand to attention. Fear skates down my back. Nchebe and my aunt are out there somewhere, and I have no idea if they're even okay. I'm not ready to face Dr Dòyìnbó . . . not without them.

Emem steps forward. 'Ọ̀gá, the ground level is compromised,' she says in a rush. 'But I believe we can still get out.'

'What about Zahrah?' I ask. She's still down on the fourth level.

Ọgá Gbénga scowls in response. 'She knows what to do.' Then he motions with his left hand and the two Òmìnira straighten. 'Let's keep it tight and fast. Move out.'

Bukola and Emem surround us, and we move into the lift quickly. It feels like hours before we arrive at the top floor, though it must have only been minutes. The doors swing apart, and I blink as smoke and bright light floods the lift. Then an energy beam bursts towards us from somewhere near where the entrance used to be.

'Get down,' Emem shouts as Bukola pulls me to the floor. I land in a confused heap, but I barely have enough time to recover before he drags me towards the now mangled DNA sculpture. Around me, agitated voices bark out commands, while above me a blue shield forms in front of Bukola. An energy beams hits it and bounces off harmlessly.

The smoke begins to clear, and I spot soldiers in a familiar-looking uniform clustered by the blown-out main entrance. I'm immediately transported back to the day those same soldiers ambushed us at Aunt Naomi's farmhouse. My vision narrows, and I'm paralysed by the memories cascading through me. Only this time I don't have Nchebe or my aunt by my side. Bukola's body strains as he protects us, and I can't see Emem anywhere.

'Time to go, Onyeka.' Ọgá Gbénga's soft voice in my ear pulls me out of my nightmare. I turn to find his grim-looking face hovering close to my own.

'What's going—?'

'No time to explain,' he interrupts. A muffled shout somewhere nearby distracts me, and I struggle to concentrate as everything becomes a jumble. 'We've got to move ... *now*.'

I look up again and see he's right. Bukola is struggling to keep the shield above us intact as it takes a pounding from the relentless energy beams. I feel a familiar tingle along my scalp and my power simmering away beneath the surface. But before I can do anything, Ọ̀gá Gbénga grabs my hand, dragging me along as he sprints away from the lobby. We race past the lifts and through a set of double doors. Ọ̀gá Gbénga turns left and opens a small unmarked grey door, revealing a narrow shaft beyond.

In one swift move, he pushes me through, clambering in after me. Then he turns to shut the door. Moments later, we hear the pounding of feet running past. The light is poor, but I make out a flight of stairs at the end of the shaft. I turn in time to see Ọ̀gá Gbénga grasp the door handle, and his hand transforms as his black diamond armour takes over. The handle buckles instantly under the pressure of his hand, the metal twisting as Ọ̀gá Gbénga pushes it back into itself until all that's left is a stump.

'We have to keep moving,' he pants, wiping the sweat from his forehead. 'That won't hold them for long.'

He shouldn't be using Ike, but we don't have much choice. We crawl through the shaft, arriving at the steep stairwell I spotted earlier. It winds downwards, back into the depths of the compound. The sound of our footsteps echoes loudly as we race down it. Ọ̀gá Gbénga leads the way, his pace punishing, and I struggle to keep up.

'Where are we going?' I pant, breathless.

'There's another way out on the fourth level. It's our only option. If we can get to the cars, then we might have a chance.'

When we reach the dimly lit garage, it's giving serious horror movie vibes. Grey concrete pillars cast a grid-like shadow across the hard ground. Electric cars in a rainbow of colours and sizes litter the vast space. We move through the maze of vehicles, keeping low, alert to any slight sound. I search the walls, looking for an exit, but find nothing.

A shaft of white light a few metres away breaks through the yellow glow of the emergency lighting, and Ọ̀gá Gbénga points towards it, a finger pressed to his lips. I immediately spy a pale grey car and the solitary figure beside it. Zahrah wears an anxious expression on her face, and her eyes dart about searching for something ... *or someone*!

'Stay here,' Ọ̀gá Gbénga whispers, and I nod, crouching low behind a pillar.

He ducks between cars with a slow, panther-like grace until the protection of the parked vehicles runs out. Then I see his shoulders straighten just before he sprints towards his daughter.

Suddenly, a grey truck appears like a silent monster from somewhere to the right of us, making a beeline for Zahrah and her car! Ọ̀gá Gbénga skids to a frantic stop as he realizes Zahrah is trapped between the two vehicles and the truck shows no sign of slowing down.

I step out of my hiding spot and sprint towards Ọgá Gbénga. It doesn't take me long to catch up to him.

'What the solar are you doing?' Ọgá Gbénga screams at me.

I have no idea, but I know I have to do something. There's no way he's going to reach Zahrah in time, and the terror on her face is all the motivation I need. The sound of Ọgá Gbénga's shout must have alerted the vehicle to our presence as it screeches into a tight turn. Smoke bursts from the massive tyres as it drifts sharply round so that it's now facing us.

Beside me, Ọgá Gbénga shifts, his diamond armour taking over his body completely.

'Get behind the pillar,' he growls, looking like a ferocious mythical creature.

Then he takes a step back as if bracing himself, and it finally hits me. He's going to try to stop it with his body. There's no way he won't be crushed!

The ominous rumble of the truck intensifies as it grows closer, and my hands begin to shake. Ọgá Gbénga is still screaming at me, but I can barely hear him above the sound of my racing heart and the roaring in my ears. Time stops and everything slows down as the truck moves closer. I can feel the ground vibrating as it nears. I peer into the vehicle and see the driver's seat is completely empty, which must mean someone is controlling the vehicle remotely. *Have the remote systems been hacked too?* Then I spot my reflection in the windscreen ... I look petrified.

That's all it takes. I harness the fear and strand after strand of hair erupts from my head, shooting towards the advancing vehicle like a thick battering ram. My hair slams through the grill and windscreen, punching its way through the centre of the truck. Shards of glass fly through the air as the truck folds round my hair and metal crunches into itself. Then the car takes flight as the momentum sends it soaring into the air.

A massive tyre breaks free, flying straight towards me. I barely have time to retract my hair as I try to create a protective shield around me, but an unexpected force sends me flying to the right. I land on the ground awkwardly, just in time to see the tyre smack straight into Ọ̀gá Gbénga. His body armour takes the brunt of the force, but the power of it sends them both spinning into one of the concrete pillars with a sick thud.

'No!'

Zahrah's scream is a raw sound of agony. Her heavy footsteps pound behind me as we both race towards her father.

CHAPTER FOURTEEN

Wiping clammy hands on my shorts, I come to a stop beside Ọ̀gá Gbénga. Luckily his armour is still in place as it's the only thing protecting him from the tyre that has him trapped against the concrete pillar. He stirs, straining as he tries to free himself.

'I'm so sorry,' I pant. 'I didn't know what else to do.'

'Hush,' Ọ̀gá Gbénga replies in a gentle voice. 'You're the reason my daughter is alive.'

I shake my head. *I'm the reason all of this happened in the first place.*

'Daddy!' Zahrah's voice is high and tight with fear as she reaches us. It's the first time I've ever heard her call Ọ̀gá Gbénga anything other than ọ̀gá or sir.

'I'm fine,' her father says. 'Help me get this thing off.'

Zahrah and I both grab the tyre and pull, but it won't budge.

I send her a worried glance, then we try again. Still nothing. Zahrah stares at her father helplessly. Her fire power can't help us. *But maybe my Ike can?* I call it forth and it answers immediately. I wrap my hair around the tyre and pull. Ọgá Gbénga cries out in pain, and I stop immediately.

'Onyeka!' Ọgá Gbénga's voice is an urgent demand and I focus on him. 'Your father is being held in a secret lodge owned by Dr Dòyìnbó inside Old Oyo National Park.' I freeze. In all the chaos I'd forgotten what Ọgá Gbénga had started to tell me just before the attack began. 'I sent the co-ordinates to the Gyrfalcon while we were in the lift. I've already verified—'

Whatever Ọgá Gbénga is about to say next is interrupted by the sound of banging somewhere behind us, and we all freeze.

'You need to find your father,' Ọgá Gbénga continues with renewed urgency. 'He's the key to fixing the serum and allowing the Òmìnira to be able to use our powers once more.'

Guilt rockets through me. I should have told Ọgá Gbénga about the serum from the very beginning. I close my eyes. It's time to tell the truth.

'There's something you should know,' I begin. 'I tried to tell you yesterday and again this morning before the attack started.'

My heart begins to pound as Ọgá Gbénga just stares at me, his gaze steady. 'Tell me now.'

I hesitate, unsure about where to start. Unsure about how

he'll react. *Will he hate me?* In the end, the words leave my mouth in a painful rush.

'Aunt Naomi fixed the serum before we found you. None of us have the disease any more.'

Zahrah recoils and I see her take several rapid swallows. A conflicted dance of emotions flits across her face. Shock, disbelief and then finally the one I was most dreading … anger. Ọ̀gá Gbénga's face is strangely expressionless.

'You've been with us for weeks,' Zahrah pushes through tight lips. 'Eating our food, using our tech, pretending to be our friends. How could you have kept something like that from us?'

I rub my arms, suddenly cold. 'I didn't know if we could trust you. We couldn't take the risk that Ọ̀gá Gbénga could turn out to be another Dr Dòyìnbó and betray us too.'

My voice cracks and an awful silence follows. Zahrah doesn't have any problem filling it though.

'Not good enough,' Zahrah yells.

'Peace, Zahrah,' Ọ̀gá Gbénga says in a quiet voice, and Zahrah throws him a disbelieving look.

'I'm so sorry,' I whisper. 'As soon as we find Nchebe and my aunt, I'll make sure the Òmìnira get the serum.'

O

Ọ̀gá Gbénga's blank expression turns quizzical. 'I can partly understand why you lied at the beginning. I might have done the same thing had I been in your position. But what I'm struggling to understand is why it's taken you so long to confess.' His voice is carefully neutral as if he's trying to make sense of me. 'What were you waiting for in order to prove we could be trusted?'

I swallow hard. How do I explain the knot in my belly that won't stop growing? How I couldn't tell the truth even though I knew hiding the serum was wrong? Would they understand the fear and distrust that Dr Dòyìnbó has left me with? But that's not the Òmìnira's fault. We're on the same side, and it's time to act like it.

'I made a mistake,' I say quietly. 'But I know now that we can trust you.'

Ọ̀gá Gbénga watches me for a long moment, and I can almost see him trying to reach a decision.

'Do you promise you'll give us the serum now?' he finally asks.

I nod. 'I promise,' I reply, in my most solemn voice.

More banging and I almost jump.

'I sealed the main doors after the explosion,' Zahrah says quickly. I throw her a worried look. It doesn't sound like they'll hold for much longer.

'We need to get him out of here,' I mutter, frowning at the tyre that won't budge.

Ọ̀gá Gbénga's face softens and a resigned look enters his eyes. 'I don't think that's going to be possible.'

'Stop talking like that,' Zahrah cries.

'It's okay,' Ọ̀gá Gbénga replies way too calmly. Then he gives me a strange look. 'I'm going to need you to do me a favour, Onyeka. You need to leave now and take Zahrah with you.'

'What?' Zahrah says, shaking her head frantically. 'No way. I'm not leaving you.'

'I can help you,' I add determinedly.

'There's no time. If you don't go now, this will have all been for nothing.' His eyes bore into mine with an urgency that scares me. 'If it's God's will, I'll find you both again, and together we'll take down Dr Dòyìnbó.'

More banging, even louder this time.

'No, Daddy,' Zahrah sobs beside me.

Ọgá Gbénga's face softens. 'You must do whatever it takes to help Onyeka find her father. Go to one of the safe houses.'

'But—'

'Promise me, Zahrah,' he commands.

'I promise,' she replies obediently, her voice wavering on the last word.

'Now go. That's an order.'

Zahrah stiffens, then her back goes proper straight. 'Yes, sir,' she says.

Ọgá Gbénga gives her a nod of approval and Zahrah grabs my arm. She marches us away from her father, her body tight with strain. I stare at her in awe, unable to imagine how hard it must be for her to walk away. Zahrah bundles me into the car before jumping in beside me. With a few taps of her communicuff, the engine starts, and she swings the vehicle round.

'Where are we going?' I gasp.

Zahrah doesn't even look at me. 'There's a tunnel that leads from the garage straight to the woods I met you in. We need to find Nchebe and your aunt. Hopefully they haven't been intercepted.'

We approach a solid wall, and the car picks up speed. *What is she doing?* Then there's a loud rumble as the wall slides apart, revealing a dark corridor beyond. I gasp. I wasn't expecting that. The minute we enter the tunnel, the doors close shut behind us and darkness closes in. Only the bright headlights of the car prevent us from being swallowed up completely.

We continue for what feels like hours in silence. I don't know what to say to Zahrah. Nothing sounds right. I know what it feels like to lose the people you love, unsure if you'll ever see them again. Sorry isn't enough. So I remain quiet, my thoughts shifting to Nchebe and my aunt. My hands clench in my lap as I pray they're safe.

Please let them be okay ... Please let them be okay ...

The words repeat over and over in my head, even as the darkness of the tunnel gives way to bright sunshine and the dense trees that border the compound. The chant continues to swirl in my mind as Zahrah repeatedly tries to contact the Gyrfalcon on her communicuff.

Please let them be okay ... Please let them be okay ...

Then at last Adanna's voice comes over the car's intercom and I'm finally able to let the words go.

'What's going on?' Adanna asks urgently. 'We received a message from Ọ̀gá Gbénga telling us to stay put with a set of strange co-ordinates included. Then all communication with the compound went dead. We've been trying to get hold of you guys for ages.'

'We were attacked,' Zahrah says. There's a sharp gasp that sounds like Aunt Naomi. 'The compound is compromised.'

'Where's Onyeka?'

It's Niyì this time, and the worry in his voice soothes something in me.

'I'm here,' I reply. 'Where are you?'

'We're fifteen minutes out.' Adanna's voice again. 'We'll be with you soon.'

'No!' Zahrah says sharply. 'We'll meet you. The further away from the compound we can get, the safer we'll be.'

The inside of the Gyrfalcon is deathly silent. We've been circling in stealth mode since Zahrah and I reached the others. It didn't take long to recount the little we knew about the attack. Zahrah explained that after the initial explosion, she'd received a message from her father instructing her to stay with her car. Somehow, through all the chaos, Ọ̀gá Gbénga was able to co-ordinate everyone and keep us safe. It makes it even worse that he's not here now.

'Wetin we go do now?' Hassan finally asks.

I jump in quickly. 'We find my father. I know where he is.'

Four sets of startled eyes swing towards me. I hadn't told them that part yet, and I quickly fill them in on everything that Ọ̀gá Gbénga told me in the garage. When I get to the bit where I confessed about the serum, all eyes turn to Zahrah with varying degrees of concern.

'It wasn't only Onyeka's decision,' Aunt Naomi finally says, stepping closer to me. 'We all agreed to it.'

Niyì nods as he and Hassan join her at my side.

'I didn't,' Adanna mutters, and I throw her an irritated look. *She's not helping!*

Zahrah's face tightens, but it relaxes seconds later. 'Are there any more secrets I should know about?'

Guilt wriggles inside me, but her words break the ice, and the tension in the jet dials down a notch. They also lock my fears about my dreams in my throat, and I swallow my confession back down.

Aunt Naomi steps towards Zahrah. 'No more secrets! Now we'd better get you dosed up if we're going to be storming secret lodges and rescuing fathers in the near future.'

'You have the serum here?' Zahrah asks quietly.

'We've got two vials leftover from the initial batch I produced. But don't worry, I can give the Òmìnira the formula so they can make more.'

Zahrah's frown is so quick that I almost miss it. She must be thinking about her father and wondering if he's safe. Then she nods once. Aunt Naomi grabs the vacuum syringe, and within moments the serum is shooting through Zahrah's body.

'Is that it?' she asks.

Adanna shoots her a small smile. 'Try your Ike.'

Zahrah raises her right hand and immediately a tiny ball of flames blooms orange in her open palm. It quickly grows into a burning orb the size of a tennis ball.

'It doesn't hurt,' Zahrah marvels, a look of wonder on her face. Her expression soon morphs into one of pure joy as the flame in her hand grows even bigger. A small giggle escapes her mouth and I can't help but smile.

This is what you've been denying them.

The words drift through my mind, turning the moment bitter, and my smile drops. But Zahrah's joy is too infectious and I feel it spreading to the others in the room, even Niyì. Then his mouth suddenly curves downwards into a worried frown. Is he thinking about his Ike? Wondering if he'll ever get it back?

He shakes his head and the frown fades. 'So Dr Dòyìnbó just owns a whole lodge in a national park and no one knows about it?'

'Knowing him, he probably bribed someone on one of the Councils,' Aunt Naomi offers. 'You need very high-level approval to build in a national park.'

'What about your mum?' Adanna asks. 'Is she there too?'

'I don't know.' My voice comes out as a small whisper. Ọ̀gá

Gbénga only mentioned my father, but I have to hope that Mum is there too. I can't even let myself think about the possibility that she might not.

'Shouldn't we make sure Ògá Gbénga is okay first?' Aunt Naomi asks. 'And then help the Òmìnira somehow?'

Zahrah straightens. 'My father's instructions were clear. Besides, we have protocols in place in case something like this was ever to happen. There are other safe houses, and everyone who's managed to escape will make their way there.' Her red eyes bore into mine. 'I promised to help Onyeka find her father.'

'How we go enter de secret lodge sef?' Hassan says with a concerned frown.

'There'll probably be a lot of soldiers,' Zahrah says, a fresh ball of fire blooming in her palm.

'What if we split up?' Adanna suggests, her forehead crinkling in concentration.

'Dat one na bad idea,' Hassan replies.

'No, Adanna's right,' Zahrah says quickly. 'We need to divide Dr Dòyìnbó's forces. What if he has Solari guarding the lodge too? They'll be tough to get past.'

I understand her plan immediately. 'A decoy?'

Zahrah nods. 'Exactly. If we can flush out the bulk of his soldiers, then maybe we can sneak in without any one realizing.'

'Na me go go. They no go see me come,' Hassan says.

'No, they'll smell you instead,' Adanna says with a snigger.

I can't help but smile as Hassan gives her a hard nudge.

'I can cover you from the air,' Aunt Naomi says. 'You might need extra fire power.'

'Okay, so that leaves me, Ada and Zahrah to find my father,' I confirm.

'What about me?' says a quiet voice.

My eyes swivel to Niyì. Somehow, in all our planning, we didn't even think to include him. Guilt pools in my belly. Just a few months ago, he would have been the one to lead this plan.

'You'll come with me, of course,' Aunt Naomi says firmly. 'I'm going to need help flying this big bird.'

There's a strained silence, and Niyì's face twists with emotions I can't pinpoint. I hold my breath, but all he does is nod and turn away.

'How do the rest of us get in?' I ask, uncertainty still clouding my voice.

A smile lights up Zahrah's face. 'I have an idea.'

CHAPTER FIFTEEN

It's late afternoon by the time the Gyrfalcon lands in a dense savannah near the edge of the national park nestled deep in Oyo Province. Adanna pointed out some of the city ruins dating back to the old Oyo Empire as we flew over the park. But we're not here as tourists today.

Adanna, Zahrah and I stay behind to continue the rest of the trek on foot, while the others head directly for the lodge to wait for us. Thankfully, the air is cooler compared to the sweltering heat earlier in the day. In each of our right ears rests an earpiece, allowing us to communicate with each other through our communicuffs. Hanging from Zahrah's and Adanna's hips are retractable grappling hooks. The kind that climbers use. I won't be needing one though.

As we move through the dense grass and thick trees, the smell of African basil, or scent leaf, as Mum calls it, wafts through the air. The strange wildlife sounds remind me that we're probably not the only hunters out and about. Luckily, we don't encounter any of the park rangers that patrol the grounds, searching for trespassers.

Soon we arrive at the co-ordinates Ọ̀gá Gbénga sent and a rocky hill looms before us. Zahrah calls it an inselberg. A dense canopy of foliage and trees covers the hill, almost hiding the four treehouse-like structures jutting from it. Three small houses sit at increasing intervals connected by narrow wooden walkways to one another and a larger main house.

They wind around the hilltop, hugging the rock face, with the smallest house sitting at the highest point. The thatched conical roof of each one looks like a dark smudge in the fading light. The only sign of life comes from the warm amber glow of light blazing from each house and the guards patrolling the walkways. The sheer number of them takes my breath away. My hands clench then open again as the daunting reality of our mission finally hits me.

We bypass the worn road leading up the hill, staying low and hidden. Instead, we hug the base of the inselberg, making our way round to the rockiest part. Jagged boulders line an almost vertical path up to the closest lodge. We stop here, waiting for our signal.

The plan is for Hassan to attack from the front via the main road and use his Ike to distract the guards, while Aunt Naomi and Niyì provide cover from above with the Gyrfalcon. The aim is that they'll lure out the bulk of Dr Dòyìnbó's forces and buy the three of us some time to sneak in from behind.

The lodges' main defences are concentrated around the biggest house, leaving the smaller houses and walkways mostly unguarded. That's our entry point. All we have to do is get past the security system and cameras, avoid all the soldiers, find my father and hopefully my mum and finally escape … *Simple, right?*

I keep telling myself everything will be fine, that no one is going to get hurt, but the churning feeling in the pit of my stomach won't quit and the negative thoughts circling my head won't quiet.

'Hassan, what's your ETA?' Zahrah says into her communicuff, making it sound like she's done this before. But I guess she did when she broke into AOS that time …

'Two minutes,' Hassan says in my ear.

'We're in position and waiting,' Zahrah confirms.

'Sweet. You go hear when we enter dia.'

The line goes dead, and anticipation and dread fills me. What if Ògá Gbénga was wrong? What if my father's not even here and we're doing all this for nothing?

'Once we move, we need to be quick. We won't have much time to find your father,' Zahrah says to me and Adanna. 'Make sure—'

The rest of her words are drowned out by the thundering blades of the Gyrfalcon as it swoops over the lodge. Niyì and

Aunt Naomi could have arrived in stealth mode, but that's not their mission. Their job is to attract attention, and they do it with style. The darkening sky lights up almost immediately as the main lodge's solar cannons fire at the black bird from hidden turrets nestled along its perimeter. Even though I know that the jet has shield tech, I can't help but hold my breath. Each hit feels like a punch to my gut.

The Gyrfalcon moves with breathtaking speed, easily dodging most of the attacks. But still I fidget with a restless need to jump in and do something.

'Not yet,' Adanna cautions, sensing my impatience.

A moment later, shouts fill the air, soon joined by grunts. Hassan has joined the party. I smile as I imagine the soldiers' confusion at their invisible enemy. My smile widens even further as I picture Hassan weaving his way through the clash of baffled guards and into the lodge unseen. That's what we're waiting for. Once Hassan has snuck in and disabled the security system, our plan is a go.

The shouting intensifies and I begin to worry. Hassan should have made it inside by now. *Something must have gone wrong.* My hair fans out around me in an agitated arc, and I take a step towards the rock face.

'Wait.'

I look at Zahrah, everything in me longing to disobey her and clamber up the wall as fast as I can. But something in her eyes stops me. A demand, loud and unspoken, blazes back at me.

Trust me.

I nod, knowing it's time to prove that I do. Just as I step back, the booming cannon fire from the main lodge comes to an abrupt stop. I look up in time to see the lights illuminating the walkways wink out as everything is plunged into darkness. *Hassan did it!*

'Now!'

Zahrah's urgent whisper acts like a starting gun and we move as one in swift silence. Zahrah and Adanna scale the rock face using their grapplers. I use my hair. I reach the walkway first, hoisting myself over the railing and onto the decking, Zahrah and Adanna following close behind me. I spy two leftover guards heading our way, and before they can clock us, my hair whips out in two lightning-fast bolts, one for each guard. They crumple to the ground, out cold. Hassan did his job well because, apart from them, it's totally abandoned up here. If all has gone to plan, Hassan should be back to causing mayhem with the guards.

I lead us upwards, following the wooden walkway, the vibrant sounds of the savannah blanketing us as we move stealthily. I scan the bushes looking for signs of movement, both human and electronic, but I see nothing in the darkness. The stillness of it all makes me nervous and a shiver skates down my spine.

This feels too easy.

Soon the imposing form of the main lodge appears before

us. It's a thick, round structure and the pointy thatched roof rises to the sky, dominating the view. A wall of glass acts as a doorway, separating us from whatever's inside. I peer through it, but I don't see anything. Just like the walkways, the building beyond appears deserted.

I glance uncertainly towards Zahrah, but she's already moving. Staying low, she approaches the glass doors, but they don't budge. She turns back to us with a confused look on her face.

'Maybe you need a code to enter?' Adanna says.

Then I spot the problem. I step forward and grasp a handle partly hidden by some foliage. Other than the solar cannons, the lodge seems pretty low tech.

With a small grunt, Zahrah steps through, moving with careful grace. It's like she's been training for this her whole life. After a moment, she turns back and motions me and Adanna inside. We follow quickly and find ourselves in what looks like a dining room.

Empty tables dot the space surrounded by clusters of chairs. Some are overturned as if the people that were sat in them left in a hurry. The temperature of the room is even warmer than the air outside and I feel sweat begin to gather on my top lip. There's no time to linger though and we cross the room swiftly, moving into a narrow hallway beyond.

There's an elevator at the end of the corridor, but we bypass it in case any guards return unexpectedly. Instead, we move up the staircase in single file. At the top we find another much wider hallway with three doors leading off it. Zahrah, still in the lead, comes to a halt, and Adanna and I join her. The doors call to us like unopened presents and my unease intensifies. We've yet to meet any sort of resistance and I don't understand why.

'Can you two dial down the fear?' Adanna grumbles. 'It stinks and I'm trying to concentrate.'

Zahrah and I look at each other.

'I don't like this. Something feels off . . .' I say, my voice low and urgent.

'Me neither,' Zahrah replies.

'We don't have time to worry. We have a job to do.' Adanna moves past the both of us, placing herself in front of the closest door. 'There's three doors and three of us.'

My eyes flick to Zahrah, and with a shrug she moves too, coming to a stop in front of the next door. With the decision made for me, I take my place outside the final door. I take a bracing breath and push it open. A wall of cardboard boxes greets me. *It's just a store cupboard!*

'In here.'

Adanna's whisper is urgent, and I turn in time to see her slip through her half-opened door. Zahrah's there first, and I follow quickly, stepping into the darkened room. An eerie feeling prickles across my skin as the details of the room begin to crystallize.

There's a small bed and a sink next to it. Beside that is a

table with a discarded tray of food sitting on top. Then I see the woman huddled in the opposite corner. I gasp and her cornrowed head lifts. Dark brown eyes stare at me from an even darker face. A face I know almost as well as my own.

'Onyeka?' the woman whispers, her voice a thin squeak of disbelief.

'Mum!' I gasp.

CHAPTER SIXTEEN

My feet are already moving and I smack straight into my mother as she's rising to her feet. Mum's arms surround me, clutching me tight ... too tight, but I don't care. For months, I've barely let myself think about her, focusing instead on my father, because somehow it seemed easier.

Thinking about Mum meant entertaining the idea that I might never see the most important person in my life again. That was a thought that was way too big for me to cope with, so I tried my best to banish her to a secret place in my mind. But now I have her back! Now I can feel her steady strength flowing into me, I can smell the spicy scent of home that's so unique to her, and it's like I can finally breathe properly again.

A deep sob breaks free, and once it starts, I can't seem to stop it. Tears spill down my face and wetness begins to slide slowly from my nose. My shoulders shake with the strength of my sobs and my chest moves as I gasp in great big gulps of air. Mum rubs my back gently and lets me cry, even as her own tears wet my skin. She murmurs soothing words of comfort every few seconds, and after a while my sobs retreat and my breathing slows down.

'Here,' Adanna says. I peek over my shoulder, and in her hand is a neatly folded tissue. 'I figured you might need it.'

I grab it with a watery smile and wipe my messy face. Then Adanna looks at my mum expectantly and I know what she's waiting for.

'Sorry, Mum. This is Adanna. I told you about her, remember?'

Mum frowns at Adanna. 'The one who was being mean to you?' she asks sternly.

Adanna's face drops. 'Erm . . .'

Oops! I totally forgot that the last time Mum and I spoke, Adanna and I weren't even friends. Mum left AOS so soon after we arrived.

'It's okay, Mum,' I cut in quickly. 'We're good now. She helped me find you.'

I quickly fill her in on everything that's happened. When I get to the part about meeting Aunt Naomi, Mum gives me a worried look. I smile back. I forgave her ages ago for not telling me I had an aunt. When I start explaining about Dr Dòyìnbó, her expression turns dark.

'I can hardly believe it,' she breathes, her voice horrified. 'Dr

Dòyìnbó was the only person I told after I made contact with your aunt. We had just started communicating through an old channel she and your father set up, and then I received a strange message that I thought was from Naomi, asking to meet. But when I arrived at the location, a big man with an even bigger forehead bundled me into a car and brought me to this lodge. I've been trapped here ever since.' Mum shudders and her arm tightens round me. 'I've been so worried about you, ókọ́ mi, praying to God to keep you safe.' Her eyes shift to Adanna. 'Clearly my prayers were answered.'

'Did you say the guy who kidnapped you has a big forehead?' Adanna asks.

Mum nods, and Adanna gives me a look I understand immediately. It must be the same man who attacked us in my father's lab and again outside Ogbunike Caves – Dr Dòyìnbó's chief goon. He's the one I've started calling Big Head.

'I'm sorry to break this up,' Zahrah cuts in suddenly, and the three of us turn towards her. I'd almost forgotten she was here. 'We need to keep moving. We've still got to find your dad.'

Mum jerks, like someone jabbed her with a pin. 'Benjamin?'

'Yeah. He's being held here,' I reply. 'It's why we came. We didn't know you would be here too, but I'm so glad we found you.' I give her a reassuring smile, but Mum looks like she's frozen.

Adanna frowns at her. 'Do you know where he is, Mrs Uduike?'

146

'I-I'm not sure,' Mum replies hesitantly. 'A few weeks ago, I overheard a guard talking about a VIP prisoner who's been here for years.'

Excitement fizzles through me. That has to be my father.

Zahrah steps forward. 'Did the guard say anything about where they're keeping this prisoner?'

Mum nods. 'There was talk of another house ... What was it he said?' Her eyes crinkle in confusion as she struggles to recall. Adanna, Zahrah and I lean closer, willing her to remember. Then Mum's face clears. 'The furthest one,' she announces triumphantly. 'That's what the guard said. He was complaining about how far he has to walk to bring the prisoner his food.'

'The smallest house at the top,' I whisper, remembering the way the buildings wound up the inselberg.

Suddenly, the crackle of static fills my ears, then Hassan's anxious voice bursts through my earpiece.

'How far?'

'We found Onyeka's mum!' Adanna replies.

'Chai!' Hassan hisses.

'But we're still looking for her dad.'

'Make you do quick,' Hassan replies. 'De guys don dey tire of me.'

I don't like the note of fear I can hear in Hassan's voice before the line shuts off. Neither does Zahrah, and she waves us forward.

'You heard him, let's move.'

Zahrah heads back to the door and steps through it into the still empty corridor, Adanna right behind her. Mum grabs my hand and, with a small squeeze, we follow them. We retrace our steps back to the messy dining room, just as the distant sound of angry shouting fills the air. Hassan was right: the guards have lost interest in him and must be returning.

'They'll probably check on your mum first,' Zahrah says with a worried look. 'It won't take them long to realize she's gone and then they'll come looking for us.'

She leads us outside, back onto the wooden walkway, and moves at a brisk pace. I look at Mum, worried she might struggle to keep up. I needn't have bothered though. Mum strides ahead, pulling me along. I'm huffing and puffing when the smallest lodge finally comes into view.

'Not so fast,' a voice calls out from behind me.

I spin round, and even though I can't see his face yet, I know the voice. It's Big Head. The pounding rhythm of feet smacking against wood erupts as soldiers join him. But when I hear the crackle of flames behind me, I turn back. Zahrah's already forming a ball of fire in her hand. I shake my head, quickly pointing to the wooden walkway beneath us. The last thing we need is to start a blaze.

We only have a few seconds before Dr Dòyìnbó's soldiers catch up with us, but it's more than enough. Power bursts through my body, and I gasp as my hair shoots out like an avenging sword. It slashes a line through the wooden decking

148

of the walkway, and the soldiers approaching come to a halt as they realize what's happening. With a deafening crack, the wood breaks apart, splintering with the force of the impact. Big Head staggers backwards, just before the wooden walkway gives way. A huge chasm, easily three metres or more, now separates Dr Dòyìnbó's soldiers and us. Big Head's face is priceless, and I resist the urge to wave at him.

'Jesu Christi,' breathes a voice behind me, and I twist to find Mum's wide-eyed gaze fixed on my hair. The last time she saw my Ike in action, I was totally not in control. I remember the fear in her eyes, and a part of me wants to hide my powers away and pretend I'm still just her little girl. Then, behind her, I see Adanna's proud grin and Zahrah's impressed face, so I lift my head, my hair spreading out around me in a glorious display of power.

'You are beautiful,' Mum gasps, her lips lifting in a shaky smile. I instantly recognize the apology behind her words. She raises a hand towards my hair, her fingers reaching for the coils still dancing in the air.

'You finished having fun?' Adanna calls out, breaking the moment. Mum's hand falters then drops.

'Yeah,' I reply with a smile. I rein my Ike back in until my hair returns to normal. 'I reckon that should hold them off for a bit.'

'How are we going to get back down though?' Adanna finally says, and the smile slips from my face.

I hadn't thought about that . . .

'We'll figure that out after we find Onyeka's dad,' Zahrah says. 'Keep moving,' she adds in a voice that makes me want to salute.

Then we're off again. It doesn't take us long to reach the entrance to the top house. It's tiny compared to the main one. Zahrah pauses, then steps back to allow me and Mum to get closer to the door. Mum doesn't hesitate. She grasps the handle with a firm grip and pushes it open.

Inside is a cold shell. In one corner is a narrow bed, and in the centre of the room is a black chair, positioned opposite a small TV. A thin man sits in the chair, watching a cartoon I've never seen before. Thick coils cascade from his head, haloing his shoulders in a tangled mess.

'Benjamin?' Mum calls out softly. 'It's me, Tọ́pẹ́. We've come to take you home.'

Then the bearded man in the chair turns his head slowly, and I suck in a sharp breath.

It *is* him!

He's both familiar and strange at the same time – a pale imitation of the vibrant man in the picture that Mum used to keep hidden in London, or the joyful photo I found in his office back in Lagos. When my father's eyes finally find us, there's no recognition. No joy or delight ... Nothing. Not even an acknowledgement that he heard Mum. He just stares at us, a blank look on his face.

I turn to Mum helplessly. She places a reassuring hand on my shoulder then steps forward, inching towards my father with slow movements as if she's trying not to spook him.

'Do you know who I am?' Mum says softly.

My father's unfocused eyes wander over her face for a long minute. For a moment, I think I see a spark of something. Then he finally speaks in a voice so rough and cracked that it sounds like it hasn't been used in a long time.

'No.'

CHAPTER SEVENTEEN

Mum gasps, staggering backwards.

'What's going on?' Adanna says, her voice sounding as confused as I feel.

'How should I know?' I mutter under my breath.

'We don't have time to figure it out,' Zahrah says urgently. 'We need to get out of here.'

'Is it bath-time?' my father says suddenly, his face as eager as a child's.

Mum looks at me, her expression unguarded for a brief moment, and I get a glimpse of the devastation there. Then she closes her eyes. When they open again, a new look I recognize drops into place. It's the same one she used to wear when she got laid off, or when she didn't have enough money left over after paying the bills to be able to buy groceries. She drops down beside my father.

'Yes, Benjamin,' she replies in a soft voice. Then, gently, almost as if my father *were* a child, she helps him out of his chair. 'We're going to run you a nice bath.'

My father nods and follows with a happy smile as she leads him out of his prison. The rest of us shuffle after them. Adanna stays close to me, and I can almost feel her trying to read my emotions. But I'm numb. This isn't how I imagined the biggest moment of my life would go. I've worried about my father being unhappy to see me again, and I've even fantasized about him being overjoyed. I never once thought he wouldn't know who I am; that he wouldn't even recognize his own family.

We don't get far down the walkway before we hear the sound of feet approaching again. Dr Dòyìnbó's soldiers must have found a way to bridge the gap somehow. *We've run out of time.* Zahrah searches frantically around us for an escape route. But there's nothing. We can't even scale the rock face again, not with my mum and father. Adanna's desperate eyes meet mine. *I can't believe it's going to end like this!*

Then a rumbling sound rises out of nowhere, shaking the wooden walkway beneath my feet, as a sleek dark shape materializes. The whirring blades of the Gyrfalcon blast the air so hard, it almost knocks me off my feet. The big bird hovers for a moment, before swinging alongside the walkway until it's parallel with us. Its massive rotary blades swing upwards, allowing the jet to get closer as the side door flies open and a figure emerges.

Niyì leans out and the cable wrapped round his waist shifts to accommodate him as he motions to us to jump. Zahrah pushes my parents in front of her and, with a mighty leap, they're in the Gyrfalcon. Then it's Zahrah's turn. Adanna tries to get me to go next, but I push her forward, and with another leap she's inside the jet.

I steady myself, ready to jump, when someone grabs me from behind.

'You're not going anywhere,' Big Head's harsh voice whispers in my ear.

I don't hesitate. I kick out like Ms Bello taught us at the academy. My foot catches his knee and he buckles, letting go of me. I scramble away just as a blast of fire whizzes past my head. It hits the walkway right between me and Big Head, setting the wood alight with a loud roar.

I hit the ground, my head ringing from the force of Zahrah's blast. There's smoke everywhere and I can barely see through the rising wall of flames. The walkway is now an inferno that's creeping up on me fast. My eyes stream as the heat grows closer, threatening to suffocate me, and the taste of ash is strong in the back of my throat. Crouching on my hands and knees, I scramble through the thick blanket of smoke, searching for the Gyrfalcon again.

I hear it before I see it, then Niyì's there, yelling something at me. I can't hear him above the roar of the blades, but his eyes meet mine and his lips move again. I concentrate hard.

Jump! He's telling me to jump.

I stagger to my feet, coughing and spluttering. I try to focus, to call on Ike, but there's too much going on and I can't concentrate. The wall of heat behind me burns even hotter, and I can barely see the Gyrfalcon now. With a shout of desperation, I fling myself into the air, hands stretched out in front of me. Niyì's face comes into focus as I soar through the sky, his frantic hands reaching for me. But it's not enough; I'm not going to make it.

Our fingertips touch, a desperate graze, and then I'm falling ... tumbling through the air in a disorientated flap of limbs. I close my eyes, trying to call my power, but I can barely control my body, never mind Ike. The ground rises up to meet me, but then something clamps around my wrist, and I come to a jarring stop. My teeth judder with the force of it and my eyes fly open to find Niyì suspended above me.

'Give me your other hand,' he shouts.

The moment I do, we shoot upwards as the long cable around Niyì's waist retracts towards the Gyrfalcon. Hassan pulls us into the jet when we reach it, then a heavy weight wraps round my neck as Adanna locks me in a bear hug.

'That was crazy,' she yells into my face.

I'm still too stunned to reply, but my eyes lock onto Niyì. A hint of the boy I knew before stares back at me. The Gyrfalcon banks sharply, and I turn to watch as the burning walkway disappears into the distance – a bright orange inferno. A flock of screeching birds races away from the destruction, just as eager to escape. As annoying as Big Head and his goons are, I can't help but hope they found a way out of there too. Even if it means we have to face them again in the future . . .

CHAPTER EIGHTEEN

The Òmìnira safe house in Lagos isn't nearly as nice as Aunt Naomi's farmhouse, but it's big and isolated, which is good, since there are eight of us now. It has enough bedrooms for everyone, including a small one Aunt Naomi is using as a makeshift lab.

It's early evening, and the five of us kids are in our usual spot, sprawled on the brown leather recliner sofa, watching a scary movie Hassan picked on the 4D holoprojector. Mum's hiding in her room, and Aunt Naomi is in the lab as usual. Adanna managed to convince me and Zahrah to hang out with her and Nchebe. I think she's trying to take both our minds off our fathers. We still haven't heard from Ọ̀gá Gbénga or the Òmìnira, and we're getting more and more worried by the day. The electric candles that Adanna lit earlier flicker on the coffee table in front of me, their glow adding a gloomy vibe that matches my mood.

It's been five days since we escaped from the lodge and since we found my parents. Mum has been worrying quietly, which is so unlike her. Her worry is usually loud. My father . . . Well, I don't actually know what his normal self is like. I can't imagine it's this though.

My father still has no idea who any of us are. He's spent the entire time since we found him sitting in the armchair in his room watching cartoons. They seem to keep him calm. Aunt Naomi says he's suffered a type of localized amnesia. She was proper upset when she first saw him. We'd hoped that he might at least recognize her, but nope, nothing.

Aunt Naomi reckons something must have gone wrong when he used his Ike to wipe his memory of hiding the serum. She thinks he somehow ended up burying *all* his memories. She's confident they're still there, and she's been working on bringing them back using her Ike. She spends several hours with my father each day, but no luck so far. She says his Ike has always been stronger than hers and it's going to take time. I heard her warning Mum to be patient yesterday. *Yeah, good luck with that.*

The house being located in Lagos was something Mum and Adanna weren't too happy about. But Zahrah says it's probably the safest place as Dr Dòyìnbó isn't likely to look for us so close to his doorstep. I should be happy I have my parents back, but instead everything feels even more complicated. My emotions are all muddled up, like a great big ball of wool, and I can't tell where one begins and another ends. I think it's why Adanna suggested we watch a movie. I know she's worried about me and how distant I've been. She still doesn't know about the dreams. No one does. I haven't had any more, and I won't let myself.

My hands squeeze the cushion in my lap just as Adanna clutches her own cushion over her face.

'Whose idea was it to watch this film?' she mutters.

Hassan laughs before reaching into the bowl of popcorn and chin chin beside him. It's a strange but tasty mix he calls popchin. Then he chucks a handful of it at her. Adanna catches some in her hand before popping it into her mouth with a triumphant grin.

'Are you two watching this, or are you just going to make a mess instead?' Zahrah grumbles, eyeing the popchin littering the ground.

Hassan rolls his eyes. 'Calm down. We go clean am.'

Zahrah opens her mouth to reply when she's cut off by a strange beeping. She frowns, then quickly looks down at her communicuff.

'Wetin happen?'

Zahrah doesn't respond, her attention completely focused on the device round her thumb. I look at Adanna and she shrugs back, equally baffled.

'It's my father.' Zahrah's voice is a hoarse croak.

Ọgá Gbénga? He's alive!

Beside me, Adanna sits up, but before we can question Zahrah, she lifts her hand towards the holoprojector. A light beams out from the communicuff, and the film playing winks out, replaced by a familiar face.

'It's good to see you,' Ọgá Gbénga says with a tired smile. 'Are you safe?'

Zahrah nods before filling him in on our location and the successful rescue mission.

'I did as you asked,' she adds.

Ọgá Gbénga's smile is full of pride. 'Well done.'

'Where are you?' Adanna asks him, interrupting their little moment.

'Safe as well. Most of us were able to escape to one of the southern compounds. A small few were captured by Dr Dòyìnbó's soldiers. I'm still working on finding out where they're being held.'

Niyì frowns at the screen. 'Do you know how Dr Dòyìnbó found the Òmìnira compound?'

I look away. I still don't know if it was my last dream and this new link to Dr Dòyìnbó that led him to us, but I daren't tell anyone about it.

'Not yet. I've not heard from my spy at the academy. I'm concerned he may have been discovered.'

Maybe it wasn't me ...

'Regardless,' Ọgá Gbénga continues, 'my main focus now is to retrieve the formula for the new serum so we can begin to produce and administer it. Then we can take down Dr Dòyìnbó and rescue the Òmìnira who have been captured.'

'I'll get Aunt Naomi straight on it,' I say.

Ọ̀gá Gbénga nods. 'I must go now.' Then his eyes move to Zahrah. 'You did well, daughter.'

Zahrah sucks in a sharp breath, and Adanna flinches beside me. Even I can feel the emotion rolling off her in painful waves. A small spark of jealousy ignites in my belly. *I wish I could talk to my father like that.* Then the projection winks out, returning to the movie we were watching just moments before.

'Are you okay?' Niyì asks Zahrah in a quiet voice. He's been making a real effort with her after the way she helped us during the rescue mission.

Zahrah's only reply is a sniff, and Niyì gives her shoulder an awkward pat. I flash her an encouraging smile. I'm really happy Ọ̀gá Gbénga and most of the Òmìnira are safe. The last few days waiting for an update have been awful, especially for Zahrah. But I also can't help but think about my father and how I may never fully get him back.

'You all right?' Adanna whispers beside me.

I swallow hard. 'I'm fine. I just need a minute.'

Adanna nods because she already understands. She and Cheyenne are the only people I never have to explain my feelings to. Sometimes they know even before I do. I glance quickly at the boys, but they're busy talking to Zahrah.

'Have you heard from Chey?' Adanna asks as I get up, almost as though she can read my mind, not just smell and hear my emotions. 'She's not replying to my texts.'

161

I pause as I try to remember the last time I texted Cheyenne. It's been a little while. Then it hits me.

'She's probably at her art camp. I think she said they're not allowed to use devices there. She called it a digital detox.'

Adanna's face screws up in horror as she tries to imagine having to live without tech. 'And she still went?'

I smile, but it quickly fades as my thoughts return to my father.

'Just go,' Adanna says. 'I don't think we'll finish the film anyway.'

With a grateful a smile, I get up. Ignoring Hassan's confused glance, I head for my room, but no amount of running away can help me block out the memory of the blank look in my father's eyes when we found him. Or the sound of Mum's tears late at night when she thinks no one can hear her.

'You're going to hurt yourself by thinking so hard, you know,' a voice says from the doorway. I sit up as Zahrah enters the room, closing the door gently behind her.

'I think I already have.' I grimace, rubbing my forehead.

'Why are you by yourself?' she replies. 'I thought the four of you did everything together?'

My nose wrinkles at her question as I try to figure out if she's being snarky. But Zahrah continues staring at me as if she's truly just curious.

'I needed some space,' I finally say.

'Is it working?'

I shrug, my fingers closing round the cowrie shell suspended from my neck. 'What are *you* doing here?'

'I needed some space,' she says, parroting my answer back at me, and I smile. 'Has that got something to do with your dad?' Zahrah adds in quiet voice, then nods towards my necklace.

My eyes snap down, startled by her observation. I didn't realize she'd noticed it, or my habit of touching it whenever I think of him.

'I always knew it would be weird when I finally met him,' I begin in a careful voice. 'But he doesn't even know who I am.' A sigh escapes. 'I guess I always thought we'd eventually get to do the fun things fathers and daughters are supposed to do.'

Zahrah shrugs again. 'I wouldn't know. You've seen how mine is.'

I go quiet. She's never talked about the strange vibe between her and her dad before. I finally gather the courage to ask the question that's been burning inside me for ages.

'What exactly happened to your mum?'

Zahrah sits down on the bed beside me, and I wonder if she'll answer.

'She died when I was eight,' she finally says. 'She refused to stop using her Ike, even though she knew the risks.'

'I'm sorry,' I say sadly.

Zahrah picks at a loose thread in the bedsheet. 'Ògá Gbénga changed after that. Then everything became about finding your father so we could cure ourselves of the disease and take down Dr Dòyìnbó.' Her voices wobbles. 'I've been training my whole life, and I've always understood my responsibilities, but sometimes I wish he'd act like my dad instead of my ọ̀gá.'

The look of longing on Zahrah's face is so stark that I turn away. It feels wrong to stare at her in this moment, like I'm intruding on something private.

'I'm beginning to realize that he was wrong about some other things too,' Zahrah adds, and I look at her in surprise. 'Nchebe aren't what I expected. I always assumed everyone from the academy was as bad as Dr Dòyìnbó.'

'They're not,' I protest quickly. 'They just don't know the truth.'

Zahrah nods. 'I get that now.' Then her expression turns thoughtful. 'Maybe when this is all over, I'll get to meet the other Solari at the academy.'

Before I can answer her, the bedroom door swings open with a loud bang. Adanna steps through, a frantic look on her face.

'You need to come now,' she gasps at me. Then she pauses, glancing between me and Zahrah. 'What were you two talking about?'

'Needing space,' Zahrah replies.

Then she looks at me, and we both burst out laughing.

'What did I say?' Adanna says.

Neither Zahrah nor I reply; we're too busy creasing up. I bend over, clutching my belly.

'Fine, don't tell me,' Adanna says crossly. 'But you'd better come. Your mum and Aunt Naomi are fighting o.'

The laughter dies in my throat, and I straighten with a jerk. *They're what?*

'Where are they?' I whisper.

CHAPTER NINETEEN

I don't fully remember the short journey back to the living room, and I arrive to find Niyì and Hassan huddled on the sofa as they watch my mum and aunt face off.

'You can't do this, Tọ́pẹ́,' Aunt Naomi says, pushing her tiny plaits off her face.

Mum's lips twist in a defiant frown and her left foot taps an impatient beat. 'Watch me.'

'What's going on?' I call out.

Both women turn at the sound of my voice. There's a guilty look on Mum's face, but it's Aunt Naomi who speaks first.

'You mother wants to return to England ... with you and your father.'

My shocked gaze switches to my mum. *Is she serious?*

Mum spreads her hands out in a defensive gesture. 'We came

to find Benjamin and a cure for your sickness. We've done both. It's not safe to stay here any longer.'

A wave of rage so fierce it almost takes my breath away washes over me. My Ike rises up and I let it, uncaring of the dismayed look on my mum's face.

'I want to stay,' I reply through gritted teeth.

'Oh,' Mum squeaks. Her shock would be funny if the situation wasn't so messed up. 'We can't,' she finally musters, a small spark of the old Mum breaking through.

The new me rises to meet it. 'I'm not leaving my friends or the other Solari.' Indecision dances across Mum's face, and the muscles in her cheek twitch as she eyes my hair. A fight is the last thing either of us needs, so I anchor my anger until my hair settles again. 'Please, Mum,' I plead. 'They need us here to help take down Dr Dòyìnbó.'

'How?' she bursts out. 'You may have superpowers, but we're not in one of your comic books. I'm not letting you get hurt or worse, God forbid.' Her voice, which has been steadily rising, ends on a harsh shout.

I know from experience that when Mum is this worked up, she's not going to hear anything I say. Usually, I'd back off until she's calmed down, but everything has changed now. I've changed.

'I know you're scared,' I begin in a quiet voice. My eyes drop to the ground, and I take a deep breath. 'But I have to help my friends.' I look up then to find Mum watching me with an intensity that's unsettling. 'I don't want to run or hide any more.' My voice cracks and my eyes burn from the tears I'm desperately holding back. 'We're going to run out of places to go.'

Mum is silent as she considers my words and, for a moment, I think she might actually listen to me. Then her expression hardens again and my heart sinks.

'I'm sorry. I've made up my mind.'

I exhale sharply as her blunt words pierce through my defences, leaving me breathless with the impact. *Why is she doing this?* I open my mouth to argue again, but Adanna's hand on my arm stops me. She shakes her head slowly, and I know then that my mum's mind is fully made up.

Frustration floods my body and Ike becomes an itch under my skin. It takes every bit of control I have to anchor it down. I can't even really be angry at Mum. I try to remember a time when she wasn't scared, but my memory doesn't go back that far. She doesn't understand what it means to be Solari and why I can't abandon the others. But, at the end of the day, she's my mum and I'm still just a kid.

I swing away before anyone can stop me, dashing past everyone.

'Onyeka!' Mum calls, but I don't stop.

I let my feet take me out of the room, past my bedroom, until I find myself outside my father's room. A soft glow peeks out from the bottom of the closed door, and I gently push it open.

Inside the room I find him seated in an orange armchair. Beside him is a small table with a glass of water and an uneaten plate of eba and efo riro. Light flickers from the TV opposite, and his eyes are glued to the images projected from it.

'Hi, Dad,' I say in a soft voice. It feels weird calling him that.

'Is it time for a bath again?' His eyes don't leave the TV, and I can't even tell if he knows I'm not Mum.

Why did I come? Whatever I'm looking for isn't here.

'No, sorry,' I reply, backing away slowly.

'Oh.'

My father turns to look at me then, and a matted clump of hair falls over his face. The rest of it hangs down his shoulders in a tangled mass of coils and kinks. I remember the photo of him I found back in London. He used to keep his hair beautifully braided and styled. Seeing the knotted tangle it's become gets to me because I know it wasn't his choice.

'I'll be back,' I tell him.

In the en-suite bathroom, I find a selection of products resting in a neat row above the sink. I eye the small bottles, knowing they'll never be enough, but after rifling through the cabinet above the sink, I find a larger bottle of leave-in conditioner. It isn't as good as Adanna's special formula, but I don't want to risk bumping into my mum. I also find a couple of clips and a spray bottle, which I fill with some water.

Back in the room, my father hasn't moved, and he doesn't even flinch when I approach. I quickly dampen his hair with a little water, add the leave-in conditioner and start detangling it section by section. My movements are clumsy at first, so I start to talk, hoping it'll calm my nerves.

'I can't believe Mum wants to leave.'

I tell him about our argument, then about the Òmìnira. As I work my way through his hair, the words pour from me, and I go on to tell him all about my adventures since coming to Nigeria. He listens with quiet patience, and when I'm done, a chunky curtain of soft twists rests against my father's shoulders. Once he gets the sides and his edges shaped up, he'll look just like he used to.

'Looking good,' I say, but his blank expression doesn't change.

I drop the last twist in my hand with a small sigh. He has no idea what I'm talking about. *He doesn't even know who I am.* Then his eyes catch the cowrie shell hanging from my neck, and he blinks slowly. He raises a tentative hand towards it, then pauses as if confused.

A shock of excitement races through me, and I pull the necklace from my neck.

'Do you recognize this?' I ask in hopeful whisper. 'It's yours.'

My father shakes his head, agitated now. 'N-no.'

'Yes.' I try putting the necklace in his hand, but he waves me away.

'It's not mine,' he snarls, and I back away instantly.

'I'm sorry . . . I just . . .'

My voice trails away helplessly. I know he can't help it, that he doesn't understand what's going on, but I can't stop the feeling of rejection flowing through me. It crashes through my control and my Ike bubbles up again. I turn away, trying to tame it so I don't scare my father.

'I gave it away,' he mutters. 'The key . . . I gave it away.'

But I'm no longer listening, lost in my own pain and disappointment. This was a mistake. *I shouldn't have come here.* My feet begin moving as I try to make my escape, then there's loud gasp behind me.

'Onyekachi?'

CHAPTER TWENTY

The floor of the hallway is hard beneath me. My bum went numb ages ago. The door to my father's room has remained closed, but I'm still sat here waiting. It's been over an hour since my father said my name and I screamed for my mum and aunt. Over an hour since they kicked me out of the room so Aunt Naomi could finish what my unplanned haircare session started. She even took my cowrie shell.

Niyì, Hassan and Zahrah went to bed ages ago. Adanna tried to get me to sleep too, but I wouldn't budge, and eventually she left me to wait alone. She said my noisy feelings were giving her a headache. I bet my curiosity sounds like a drum – probably an entire festival full of them.

Well, I'm done waiting. I stand before I can change my mind, moving in front of the door. *Should I knock?* I wonder, before quickly shaking the thought away. What if they tell me to go away? Instead I take a deep breath and open the door to peek in. Mum and Aunt Naomi are sat on the bed, and between them is my father, perched on the edge.

He's talking to Mum, but he hasn't seen me yet.

'You know about Dr Dòyìnbó?' my father says, his voice cracking.

Mum nods. 'Yes. Naomi already explained this.' Then she turns to my aunt. 'What do you think happened?'

Aunt Naomi frowns. 'There are a lot of memories and emotions tied to this cowrie shell. Benjamin left it for Onyeka, used it to protect the lab and its secrets, and he even made it the key to finding and unlocking the serum.' She holds up the shell to the light. 'Seeing it and her together probably caused a big enough shock to weaken the memory block he placed on himself with his Ike, which allowed me to break through it completely.' She looks at my father in wonder. 'I should have thought of it earlier. The cowrie shell has always been the key.'

'What about the serum?' my father asks suddenly. 'It's not safe. I couldn't fix it in time.'

'Naomi's figured it out,' Mum says gently, even though I can tell she's tired.

My father goes still, then he looks at his sister with a slow, disbelieving shake of his head. 'So we're free from the disease?'

Aunt Naomi straightens, and her chin lifts. 'Yes. We won't lose Ike, Ben. It's going to be okay.'

I finally step into the room as my father breathes out a long sigh.

'Thank God,' he whispers. Something must have alerted him to my presence because he stiffens, and his head swings my way. Then his whole face softens.

'Onyekachi.'

Warmth floods my belly as the sound of his voice washes over me. No one has ever said my name like that, with such satisfaction. On his lips, my name almost sounds like a blessing. Then a smile lights up his entire face, and in two giant strides he's in front of me. My mind goes blank for a moment before I quickly drop to both knees in the traditional Yoruba greeting that Mum drilled into me. Then I remember that my father is Igbo.

'Ǹdéèwō,' I greet him, using a little of the Igbo language Adanna taught me. Big hands pull me up and into a hug. As he strokes my hair, I relax for the first time in days. He releases me and steps back.

'Nwa m nwanyi,' *My daughter*. Then my father circles me slowly. 'Let me look at you.'

His eyes are bright with unshed tears as they drink me in, and I study him back in return. I wonder what he sees. I was so little when he last saw me. *Am I what he expected?*

'Kèdú kà í mèrè?' *How are you*. His voice is not quite steady.

'I'm fine,' I reply, my voice wobbly too. He lifts my chin with his forefinger. 'Really,' I add.

'I'm late,' he says, switching back to English. 'I should have been here years ago.'

My throat tightens and I swallow, pushing the tears back down. 'It's okay.'

'You must have questions.'

That's exactly what Aunt Naomi said when I met her for the first time, and I'm reminded that they're twins.

'I don't even know what to call you,' I finally burst out, just as I replied all those months ago.

He smiles then. 'How does Papa sound?'

I nod slowly. It sounds good.

A few hours later, I'm with Papa in his room again. He got tired after meeting everyone. I'd already updated Aunt Naomi about Ògá Gbénga, and she promised to send the formula as soon as possible. She also gave Papa the last of the new serum, but I don't think he'll be using his Ike any time soon.

'Your friends seem very nice,' Papa says.

Everyone was so excited to meet him, especially Adanna. She was totally fangirling over him and asking loads of questions about his genetic research. But Papa couldn't remember, and he kept forgetting people's names, even Aunt Naomi's. She reckons his memory will stabilize over time.

'How much do you remember?' I ask curiously.

Papa taps the end of my nose. 'The important things. I

know who my family is and how I feel about them. There *are* patchy spots, like my childhood, moments with your mother . . . your birth.'

There's a sadness to the smile he gives me, and I want to give him a hug and tell him everything will be okay.

'I'm sure it will come back,' I say instead.

Papa shrugs, then a resigned smile replaces the sad one. 'It's a small price to pay to have kept the serum safe.' He pats my hand gently. 'I'll enjoy making new memories to replace the forgotten ones.'

I smile back. Then Papa picks up something from the bedside table. 'I have something for you.' He places it on the bed between us, and a glint of metal catches my attention. Then I see the delicately engraved silver box, but it's faded, now barely shimmering under the soft lights.

'I hope you can forgive its sad appearance. Naomi assures me it has never left her side. I gave it to your aunt for safekeeping many years ago. Before Dr Dòyìnbó . . .' His voice trails off and he swallows hard, like it's painful to remember. 'I hoped one day I'd be able to give it to you.'

Curiosity kicks in and I open it. A clear, bright melody immediately plays. It's a music box! As I open the lid further, a beautiful silver fairy comes into view. She spins slowly in place to a simple tune, her delicate wings flaring out behind her. She looks as if she's about to take flight. As she turns, I fall in love, and I look up to find Papa watching me intently.

'It's an Aziza,' he says. 'It belonged to my mother.'

'It's beautiful,' I breathe, my eyes drifting down to the music box again. 'Dàalụ, Papa.' *Thank you.*

He nods as I gently close the lid, my fingers drifting over the metal surface. Papa clears his throat and my fingers still.

'You're so grown – a young lady now. I've missed so much.' I frown at his sudden change of topic. 'I don't know your favourite colour or what music you like to listen to. I don't even know what your future career plans are.'

I blink at him. *He wants to know my career plans?* I should be used to it though. Cheyenne's dad is like this too. Even at our age, Cheyenne and I know the drill. We're expected to finish school with good grades, then get a good job that pays well. But everything has changed. *I have superpowers now.* My future feels too uncertain, and if we don't stop Dr Dòyìnbó, I'm not even sure if I'll have one.

'I've been Solari for, like, five minutes,' I finally reply. 'I don't think I can use Ike in an office.'

Papa gives a small laugh. 'Yes, I can imagine that has taken some getting used to.'

'You could say that.'

His laughter dies suddenly. 'I wanted more than this for you. A better future. A proper legacy.' I look away, my throat tightening with unshed tears. 'I'm sorry,' Papa says, seeing my distress. 'I don't mean to overwhelm you.' His large hand covers mine. 'I have so many things to catch up on. There's so much to learn about being your father.'

'You're here now,' I manage to croak.

Papa nods and places a hand on my head, his gaze sharpening on my hair. 'Your mother explained what your Ike is. Will you show me?'

I nod and call it forward. It answers easily and my hair flares out around me. Something feels different though. I trace the bonds of my anchor, finding Nchebe and Mum straight away. But there's a new connection. I follow it eagerly, but I already know who I'll find.

'You are spectacular,' Papa breathes, and an overwhelming sense of pride tingles through me. 'I always wondered what your Ike would be, and I'm so glad that you get to keep it. That I didn't take that away from you.'

So am I. It hasn't been easy learning to accept my power, but I can't imagine being without it now. It's why seeing Niyì struggle without his Ike is so hard to watch. The fact that Papa made the serum that caused the problem in the first place makes it so much worse. The joy fuelling my power subsides and my hair falls back into place.

'Why didn't you go to the Councils or tell Mum the truth?' I ask, desperate to understand.

Papa looks away, but he doesn't pretend not to know what I'm talking about.

'After I discovered the truth about Dr Dòyìnbó, I panicked. He's incredibly powerful, so I was certain he'd come after me if he found out I knew, and I was right. When I realized the serum I created removed Ike, I tried my best to fix it, but there wasn't enough time.' His voice deepens. 'I thought the less you and your mother knew, the safer you'd be.'

I step back from the bed, my hands lifted. 'But we weren't. We walked right into Dr Dòyìnbó's trap.'

Papa flinches at the sharpness of my tone. 'I'm sorry. It's a poor answer, but it's all I have. I did what I thought was best.'

His reply makes me pause. *Haven't I been doing the same thing? Keeping secrets?* When I don't say anything, Papa sighs heavily.

'I'll always live with the knowledge that I failed both the people I love.' Papa stares at me, his voice solemn. 'I didn't protect you and your mother, and I wasn't there when you needed me most. But I promise you I'm here now, and I'll do whatever it takes to make things right.'

I struggle to hold his stare, but Papa's earnest expression doesn't waver. I step closer until we're within touching distance again, and I give him a tentative smile. He blinks rapidly and looks away.

'There is something . . .' I begin slowly.

'What?' he replies eagerly.

I quickly explain about Niyì and the missing data in his digital pad. Aunt Naomi hadn't told him that part yet because she didn't want to overwhelm him.

'We need your help,' I finish in a rush.

Papa places a hand on my shoulder and gives it a small squeeze. 'Whatever it takes.'

CHAPTER
TWENTY-ONE

Papa gets to work straight away, much to Mum's annoyance. He's spent the last two days camped out in the lab with Aunt Naomi. Mum keeps going on about him needing to rest, but I think she's only saying that because she was hoping to spend more time with him. At least Papa was able to convince Mum that we can't go back to England because we're needed here. Especially now the Òmìnira have the formula for the serum and have started making more.

Papa and Aunt Naomi have been testing and prodding Niyì so much that he's even crankier than ever. Adanna's been keeping me, Zahrah and Hassan updated, and I can tell that she's loving the chance to learn from my dad and aunt.

It's now been seven days since we arrived at the Òmìnira safe house and it's late in the afternoon. Hassan's got Zahrah watching some cheesy action movie, and Mum is braiding my hair. She still can't get over how much easier it is to do now. She's convinced it's because of Adanna's conditioner, but I know it's really because she's stopped seeing my hair as a problem. I don't tell her that though.

'Chai, I'm never watching anything with you again,' Zahrah says with a grimace as the movie ends. 'You always pick rubbish movies.'

Hassan laughs, throwing an oversized cushion at her. I look away with a smile, tuning out their harmless bickering. Then Adanna rushes into the living room, her locs loose around her shoulders.

'We did it!' she says, holding up Papa's digital pad. 'Your dad and aunt are brilliant!' Adanna finishes in a rush.

I rear up suddenly and wince. I forgot Mum was doing my hair.

'Stop moving,' Mum grumbles, and I freeze.

'What are you talking about?' I ask Adanna, trying not to move my head.

Adanna's practically jumping up and down now. 'It was actually so simple. All this time we've been trying to undo the effects of the original serum, but your father realized that we needed to focus on trarium instead and how it causes the mutation in the first place. So we replicated that effect and reactivated Niyì's Ike.'

I stare at Adanna blankly, not quiet believing what she just said.

'Eh?' Hassan asks, echoing my disbelief.

'I think she just said that they figured out how to get Niyì's Ike back,' Zahrah says in a quiet voice.

I leap off the sofa, ignoring Mum's loud cry and my stinging scalp, and rush over to Adanna.

'Seriously?'

She nods, a huge smile spreading over face. 'He's back.'

He did it! Papa did it. Hassan bolts from the room with Mum and Zahrah close behind, but I hesitate and Adanna gives me a strange look.

'Aren't you coming?'

I want to, but my feet don't seem to want to co-operate. *What do I even say to Niyì?* Adanna nudges me forward, totally in tune with my feelings.

'It's Niyì,' she whispers into my ear.

She's right, and my feet begin to move again. By the time we get to the lab, Hassan and Niyì are already talking but stop when they see me.

'Hi,' I say shyly.

My nervous fingers tangle into the loose curls resting against my shoulders.

Niyì rubs his head. 'I got my Ike back.'

'I know.' My eyes follow the movement of his hand. 'How do you feel?'

Niyì shrugs. 'Like I used to, but different too . . .' He pauses and looks away. 'I'm probably not making any sense.'

'This is the most sense you've made in weeks,' Adanna mutters.

Niyì frowns at her. 'I haven't been that bad.' Then his forehead wrinkles. 'Have I?'

I open my mouth to reassure him, but Adanna's faster.

'You've been an unbearable donkey.'

Niyì blinks like he can't believe what Adanna's just said. Then he's laughing, and soon the rest of us are too. Except for Zahrah, who stays still, watching us.

'We'll leave you all to talk,' Aunt Naomi says with a pointed look at Papa and Mum. Then the three of them leave the lab.

'We tink say we no go have you back again,' Hassan says after a moment.

Niyì looks down. 'Me too. Without Ike, everything felt wrong, and no matter how hard I tried, I couldn't figure out how to feel right again.'

'Chai,' Hassan whispers.

'It felt like you guys didn't need me any more,' Niyì continues. 'Like I didn't belong in Nchebe without my powers.'

I move closer to him. 'That's not true.'

Niyì gives me a look. 'Really? You stopped listening to any of my ideas.'

'That's because your ideas were terrible,' Adanna replies, rolling her eyes. 'If we'd stormed AOS, we'd all be finished by now!'

Niyì gives her a dirty look. 'Fine. But how about the mission to rescue Onyeka's parents? You guys left me behind for Aunt Naomi to babysit.'

There's total silence. Okay, fair enough, we did totally do that. But it was a dangerous mission, and I tell him as much.

'I know that,' Niyì says in a dismissive tone. 'But I'm still a member of this team, even without Ike.'

'Bros, make you no vex. You know say we be Nchebe for life!' Hassan slaps Niyì on the back. 'Notin spoil.'

'I'm sorry too,' Adanna says. 'We're supposed to be a team, and I guess I forgot that.'

All eyes turn to me, but I stay silent. A part of me understands what Niyì is saying, but we were only trying to keep him safe. Without Ike, it's much easier for us to get hurt.

'You don't get it, do you?' Niyì says.

'I want to,' I reply. 'But I'm not going to apologize for looking out for you.'

There's a really awkward silence as Niyì and I lock eyes in an epic stare-down that neither of us is willing to back away from.

Niyì's jaw tightens and his hands clench into fists by his side. 'Do you remember how you felt when you first discovered we were Nchebe and I didn't understand why Dr Dòyìnbó got you to join our mission?' I nod. It's been months since that moment, but I can remember my anger like it was yesterday. 'That's how I've been feeling since I lost my Ike,' Niyì finishes.

There's a sudden tightness in my throat and I look away as understanding finally dawns. I hated it when I thought Niyì saw me as useless and untrustworthy because I couldn't control my powers. But underneath the anger was hurt too. I wanted so badly to belong, and it felt like he was shutting me out for a reason I couldn't help.

I can't believe I made Niyì feel like that.

'I'm sorry,' I say softly. 'You never stopped being one of us.'

Niyì nods. 'I know that now. Whatever happens with my Ike, I know who I am.' Then he holds out his hand, letting it hang in mid-air. I stare at it for a moment, then reach out and pull him into a hug. Niyì is stiff at first, then his body relaxes. It feels good to have him back.

He pulls away, and Hassan is there too with his own hug. Then it's Adanna, but she just holds out her hand. Niyì takes it with a sly smile.

'Hey,' she yelps, letting go of his hand. It takes me a moment to clock that Niyì must have zapped her with his ice Ike. 'What was that for?' she grumbles, rubbing her frosty fingers.

'Because I can,' Niyì says simply, and Adanna grins back after a moment. Then his gaze swings to me. 'I guess you were right about my anchor being the academy.'

Before I can reply, Niyì turns his attention to Zahrah, who's still hovering by the door. *Has she been watching us this whole time?*

'I owe you an apology. I wasn't exactly the nicest to you at the start.'

Zahrah shrugs. 'I did wonder if that was just your personality,' she says, and Adanna sniggers. 'But now I think

I understand you all a bit better. You're not as bad as Uche thinks you are.'

Niyì grimaces. 'Thanks . . . I think.' Then he clears his throat. 'Look, I know I haven't been fair to you or your dad. Without your help, I wouldn't have had any hope of getting my Ike back, so thank you.'

Zahrah's eyes widen. I don't think she was expecting him to say that. 'It was nothing. We're on the same side after all.'

Niyì holds his hand out to Zahrah, and she eyes it warily.

'I won't zap you too,' he says.

Zahrah's expression doesn't change. 'Yeah, but when was the last time you washed your hands?'

Niyì's mouth falls open and there's a moment of stunned surprised. Then he starts laughing. It quickly spreads, and soon we all join in. Even Zahrah. For one precious moment, I'm able to forget about Dr Dòyìnbó. My family is complete, and my world is whole again. It feels good.

CHAPTER
TWENTY-TWO

I could get used to waking up to the smell of akara. The spicy, warm aroma fills the house. As I approach the partly opened kitchen door, the sound of my parents' voices greets me, and I hesitate. But curiosity gets the better of me, and I move quietly, peeking into the room.

The glossy black units and matching steel accessories look like they belong in a restaurant. The only thing remotely homely is a large augmented digital picture of a forest hanging on the wall opposite the dining table. Every few seconds, the trees sway in an imaginary wind.

I spot Mum by the cooker, dressed in a simple skirt with a T-shirt tucked into it. Her face is bare, and her coils are woven into a threaded style, the thick branches of hair weaving in and out in a maze-like design. She looks like a teenager. Mum doesn't really need make-up. Her clear, smooth skin always gleams like one of the stolen bronze Benin masks I saw in the British Museum once. I find Papa by the sink, washing some dishes.

Mum moves from the counter, passing Papa, and his hand flashes out and grabs her arm. She comes to an abrupt stop, a small frown on her face. Her eyes drop to my father's, and a long look passes between them. Slowly my mum's face softens, her beautiful lips parting slightly. Papa's hand on her arm moves upwards and I quickly step forward. I don't want to see what comes next.

'Good morning,' I say quickly, trying to act like I didn't just witness some kind of moment. *Are they're getting back together?*

'Did you sleep well?' Papa asks me, and I nod.

It doesn't take long for the amazing smell of Mum's cooking to bring everyone out of hiding. Hassan and Niyì show up first, and Adanna and Zahrah aren't too far behind them. Aunt Naomi joins us last. Luckily, Mum put a plate aside for her. Hassan and Zahrah can really pack it away. I swear they have three stomachs each.

Our loud voices fill the air as multiple conversations battle it out for supremacy. Niyì and Hassan are winning with their stupid argument about whether chin chin is better than puff puff when Zahrah's communicuff starts beeping again. The room goes silent, and she looks down at her hand.

'It's a call from Bukola,' she says with a frown.

I straighten when I hear the name of the Òmìnira who used

to guard Ọ̀gá Gbénga's quarters. No one's heard from him since the attack on the compound. We thought he must have been one of the ones captured.

'Maybe he escaped and couldn't get in touch until now?' I say.

Zahrah gives me a doubtful look and I understand immediately. Something feels off.

'Don't answer it,' Aunt Naomi whispers.

Zahrah looks torn. 'I have to. Bukola might need our help.'

Still, she hesitates, as if she's waiting for permission. I get it. For the first time, she doesn't have her dad around guiding her, or her people supporting her. But we're here.

'Do it,' I tell her.

Beside me, Adanna nods. Mum even reaches over and pats Zahrah's hand. Zahrah swallows once, then she points her communicuff towards the digital picture on the opposite wall. A light beams out from it and the picture of the forest winks out. Then the screen bursts into colourful life, and the face from my dreams fills the screen. Except this time, he's real.

Dr Dòyìnbó's bushy brows look even bigger than usual, and they lift into his hairline as a smirk fills his face. His pink shirt clashes horribly with a yellow bow-tie, and behind him I spot the familiar walls of his office. He raises his hand and waves, the black communicuff around his index finger flashing ominously.

Did he capture Bukola? That's the only way he would have got access to his communicuff.

'I hope I haven't caught you at a bad time,' Dr Dòyìnbó drawls.

'Let me catch you!' Mum hollers. 'I will finish you for what you've done to my family.'

'Oh, Tọ́pẹ́. Still so quick to jump into things you have no clue about.'

If Mum could jump into the screen and knock him out, she fully would. As it is, Papa is barely able to hold her back.

'Don't you dare talk to my wife like that,' Papa says, his voice bubbling with fury.

'Is that any way to greet an old friend, Benjamin?' Dr Dòyìnbó smiles.

'You're no friend of mine,' Papa replies sharply.

'That wasn't always the case, but I'll ignore your hostility for now. It's your daughter I'm more interested in.'

Every eye turns to me.

'You leave my daughter alone!' Mum screeches, grabbing me close.

Ordinarily I'd be totally embarrassed by Mum's antics, but I'm grateful for it right now as fear floods me. I let her wrap her arm round me. Dr Dòyìnbó completely ignores her though.

'Hello, Onyeka,' he says softly, and I tense at the sound of his smooth tone. 'It's so good to see you again.' The pleasantness of his greeting takes me aback. This is the man who has tried to destroy my life, yet listening to him, you'd think we were besties. 'Congratulations on that daring rescue.'

Am I supposed to say thank you? I wouldn't have had to rescue my parents in the first place if it wasn't for him.

'What do you want?' I demand. 'You never do anything without a reason.'

Dr Dòyìnbó's face lights up with a broad smile. 'Very true, Onyeka,' he replies. 'I should probably start by thanking you all for the treasure trove of data you left behind at Naomi's farmhouse. It made for some very interesting reading.'

My heart begins to race. *Please not the serum...* Adanna tried to fry as many hard drives as she could, but what if she missed a vital one?

'Well done, Naomi. I always suspected you were smarter than your brother.'

'Oh God,' Aunt Naomi gasps. 'He knows.'

'Of course I know. Did you really think you could keep something so important from me?' A hard look comes over Dr Dòyìnbó's face. 'I want the new serum.'

'No way,' I push out through tight lips. 'There's no chance we're giving it to you.'

'That's where you're wrong. You see, after I discovered its existence, I thought we'd be able to agree to a simple exchange,' Dr Dòyìnbó says. 'Your parents for the formula. But after your escapade at my lodge, I've had to change tactic.'

The view on the screen pans to the left suddenly and Dr Dòyìnbó disappears from view. In his place is Big Head, a huge smirk decorating his face. But I barely notice it as my attention is grabbed by something way worse.

Why is Cheyenne on the screen?

It takes a moment for my brain to catch up with my eyes; to understand what Dr Dòyìnbó has done. Cheyenne's short fro halos her face, the furry fox ears she always wears peeking out from the tangled mass, and her eyes are red and puffy from crying. Fury ripples through my body and I lurch towards the screen. Only Mum's hand on my shoulder halts me from trying to jump into it.

How does he know about her? Then I remember my first time in HOME, the Holographic Offensive Multisensory Environment back at the academy. It's where I told Dr Dòyìnbó about Cheyenne. I slump back. I did this. *This is all my fault.*

'How about a new trade instead?' Dr Dòyìnbó says as he returns to the screen. 'Your friend was surprisingly easy to acquire from her little camp. A forged message and they all think she's homesick and has returned to London early.'

My mind whirrs at what Dr Dòyìnbó's done. Cheyenne's parents must still think she's at camp. Chey must be bare angry though. She's probably more upset about missing art camp than she is about being kidnapped.

'I tire of this game and all the fighting. This time, you will come to me. Give me the formula for the new serum and Cheyenne can return home,' Dr Dòyìnbó continues. My stomach drops as his plan becomes clear. 'Or is she expendable now you've found some shiny new friends?'

'You're a monster,' I cry. First his awful bargain for my parents' safety and now this.

'Why? Because I'm willing to do whatever it takes to save this country?' Dr Dòyìnbó's expression turns knowing. 'You, of all people, should understand that desire, Onyeka.'

I swallow and look away. He's talking about the dreams. Even though I knew the risks, I didn't shut them down because I was so desperate to find my parents.

Adanna's staring at me now. 'What is he talking about?'

Dr Dòyìnbó won't shut up though. 'You should be asking *who* she's been talking *to*.'

Every eye is on me now and my throat feels even drier. The truth has finally caught up with me.

'I had more dreams,' I finally whisper. 'Before we reached Kano, and again at the Òmìnira compound. Dr Dòyìnbó was in all of them.'

Adanna rubs her eyebrow. 'That's not possible. Aunt Naomi showed us how to stop the dreams.'

'I didn't mean to let him in,' I mumble, but Adanna gapes at me like she doesn't know who I am any more. 'It wasn't until the last dream that I found out there was a link between us that meant he could trace my location. I was just trying to help.'

'By talking to *him*?' she hisses. 'I thought we said no more secrets.'

'Thank you for your help, Onyeka,' Dr Dòyìnbó cuts in, adding more pepper to my problems. 'I've been searching for Gbénga and his band of Rogues for many years.'

Aunt Naomi gasps and my stomach sinks as the full extent

of my final secret is revealed. So the attack on the Òmìnira *was* my fault. Now Niyì and Hassan are staring at me like I've grown a second head, and Zahrah … she won't even look at me. My mum and dad just look bare confused. Dr Dòyìnbó, the little snitch, laughs as if he didn't just throw a bomb into my life and watch it detonate. I guess our so-called link no longer matters now he knows about the new serum.

'I'm not a cruel man,' Dr Dòyìnbó adds silkily. 'I'll even let go of the Rogues I captured. I'll let you all go. But only if you leave this country and never return. Nigeria and the Solari are mine.'

'We don't belong to you,' Zahrah hisses at the screen.

'Yeah,' Niyì adds. 'You've been knowingly letting us die for years, and you told everyone we're traitors. But now you're letting us go … ? Do you really think we're going to trust anything you say?'

Dr Dòyìnbó's face evens out. 'You don't really have a choice—'

'Ọ̀gá Gbénga will never agree to this,' Zahrah cuts in before he can finish.

I stare at her. She's right. Ọ̀gá Gbénga will never agree to us giving Dr Dòyìnbó the formula for the new serum. Not even to save Cheyenne. There's too much at stake. If Dr Dòyìnbó is able to use the serum, he'll finally have his army of Solari to take over Nigeria. I don't even want to think about how many Solari would be hurt either trying to help or harm him.

'Gbénga won't be able to stop me,' Dr Dòyìnbó says bluntly.

'There's barely any of you Rogues left and not enough of you can use Ike to be a real threat.'

Zahrah doesn't even flinch at the cruel taunt, and I know why. Dr Dòyìnbó hasn't clocked yet that the Òmìnira have the new serum; that they're powerful again.

Dr Dòyìnbó's mouth stretches into a persuasive smile. 'Don't take too long as I won't be able to guarantee young Cheyenne's safety for ever. Do consider my deal carefully. I could easily wait for Onyeka to dream again and send my men after you, but this way no one gets hurt.'

The screen goes black again, leaving behind an awful silence that lasts about a minute before several voices erupt at the same time.

'We're not seriously going to give him the serum, right?'

'Dat man tie e, too ugly o.'

'We have to rescue poor Cheyenne.'

I ignore Niyì and Hassan, focusing instead on Mum's declaration. Cheyenne is the only thing I'm interested in talking about right now.

'We can use the serum as bait,' I suggest as a plan begins to form. 'Pretend we're going to give it to him.'

'That could work,' Zahrah replies, looking at me reluctantly. 'Then we can rescue my family and your friend without risking the serum.'

'Did you bang your head in those dreams you forgot to tell us about?' Adanna snaps. 'Dr Dòyìnbó will never fall for that.

Besides, he'll want proof the formula is real before he hands Chey over.'

'Then we give it to him,' I reply, ignoring the anger in her tone. 'We can always destroy it after we get Cheyenne back.'

Papa shakes his head. 'Under no circumstance can we risk Dr Dòyìnbó getting his hands on the formula. What if something goes wrong?'

I turn to Zahrah, my voice pleading. 'The Òmìnira will help us, right? Ọ̀gá Gbénga said he'd be ready soon.'

Zahrah shakes her head. 'Not for a few more days; they're still distributing the last of the serum. Besides, there's no way Ọ̀gá would agree to such a risky plan.'

'She's my best friend.' I'm practically yelling now.

Zahrah glares at me. 'The Solari at the compound are my family and you put them in dange—'

'Our priority is to get somewhere safe,' Papa cuts in. 'We'll figure out how to save Cheyenne after that.'

'There's no other way,' I cry. 'You heard Dr Dòyìnbó. He's going to hurt her.'

'He won't,' Papa insists. 'Not while we still have the serum.' Then his expression turns stern. 'We'll discuss your dreams and why you didn't tell us about them later. Right now, we need to get out of here. Once Dr Dòyìnbó realizes he's not getting that serum, it's only a matter of time before he comes after us.'

I turn to Niyì, my eyes begging him to back me up.

'I agree with your dad,' he says softly. 'We can't risk it.'

I scan each face, looking for someone who'll help me, but no one does because it's my own fault that I lied and put us in this situation. Now no one trusts me. A part of me knows that they're right, and that the serum is too dangerous to risk, but the other part of me remembers each and every moment Cheyenne saved me in some small or big way. And now, because of me, she's in danger. I have to fix it!

A new plan begins to form. Adanna's eyes swing towards me, but I refuse to meet her gaze this time. Mum tries to put her arm round me and I push it off. Soon everyone's talking again, making plans for our escape. No one notices as I leave the room. Their discussion is pointless to me now because there's no way I'm abandoning Cheyenne. If we can't *give* Dr Dòyìnbó the serum, the only option left is to *take* Cheyenne back.

CHAPTER
TWENTY-THREE

I'm barely three steps into my room before Adanna slips in behind me, shutting the door behind her. I expected anger, but the wariness on her face hits like a punch to my belly.

'Whatever you're planning, stop it,' she says, her voice tight with worry.

I ignore her and keep moving until I reach the bed. 'He's got Cheyenne,' I finally reply before throwing myself down.

Besides Mum, Adanna's the only other person who understands what Cheyenne means to me.

She plops down next to me on the bed. 'I know, but that doesn't mean you should put yourself at risk again.'

I frown at her. *Why is she being so understanding?* I've been hiding the truth about the dreams from her and everyone else, and my stupid mistake led Dr Dòyìnbó to the Òmìnira. She should be cussing me out. It's what I deserve.

Adanna must smell my confusion because she pats my leg awkwardly. 'It's not like I haven't made my own mistakes in the past.'

Yeah, but none as big as mine …

'Chey's in danger because of me,' I push out through gritted teeth. 'Now everyone wants me to just leave her and hope for the best?'

'That's not what your dad said, and you know it,' she snaps at me, and the force behind the words shocks me into silence. 'He just asked you to wait so we can come up with a plan that doesn't mean giving Dr Dòyìnbó even more power.'

I cross my arms, my nostrils flaring. 'What's the point of being Solari if I can't use my powers to help the people I care about?'

Adanna sighs. 'We're powerful, yes, but we're not invincible. We stick together because that's how we stay safe.'

I know Adanna's right, but the knot in my belly won't let me admit it. The need to make sure Cheyenne is all right is like a force, propelling me forward. Beneath it is another need too. I need to fix my mistake.

'I hear your emotions all the time,' Adanna continues, her eyes blazing at me. 'It's like you've got your own theme tune following you everywhere. But I never hear joyful melodies any more.'

My shoulders droop as a tremor enters my voice. 'I don't want anyone else getting hurt because of me.'

'What are you talking about?'

'Everyone I love ends up hurt. Look at my mum, Niyì and now Chey.' I throw up my hands. 'Even my dad lost his memories trying to protect me.'

The fire in Adanna's eyes dims a little. 'There's that guilt again. Why are you so determined to blame yourself for everything?'

'Because it *is* my fault.' I cover my eyes with my arm, suddenly tired.

'Then it must be my fault Dr Dòyìnbó managed to fool us.' Adanna yanks my arm away, refusing to let me hide. 'I should have been able to sense his true intentions, right?'

'That's so stupid,' I tell her. 'You couldn't have known.'

Adanna gives me a smug look and I roll my eyes. *I walked right into that again.*

'Our emotions fuel Ike and it's really easy to let them take over. I should know. But you have to stop letting them control you like this.'

Her words are like a lifeline, and I desperately want to grab onto them. But my fear won't let me. *You did this.* The words whisper through my mind and my jaw tightens. *Now fix it!*

Adanna's eyes narrow with suspicion. 'You're going to try to save Chey by yourself, aren't you?'

'I don't have a choice,' I tell her. 'Chey would do the same for me.'

I remember the first time I met Cheyenne in after-school

200

club on my first day. We'd been making Father's Day cards and I'd drawn a picture of my mum. The teacher asked me about my dad, and embarrassment and anger flooded me because I couldn't answer her. My emotions began to swell. I'd just started to use my Fibonacci trick when a high and steady voice cut into my thoughts, distracting me from my counting.

'I like your drawing,' the voice said.

The confidence in it confused me. Even more confusing was the way the rage burning inside my chest lowered to a quiet anger in response. I turned round to find a tiny girl with two Afro puffs and furry fox ears standing there. Her smile was so big I swear it made her eyes sparkle.

'I like your hair too. It's different,' the girl said in that same steady voice.

I eyed her suspiciously. No one *ever* talked to me first. Mama used to say it was because most people are like sheep – they stick with what they know.

'I'm Onyeka,' I finally said.

'I know,' she replied, and I frowned in response. Her smile dropped and she nodded towards my hair. 'You're kind of hard to miss.'

There was nothing mean in her voice, only truth, and in that moment I knew I could trust her.

'Yeah, I guess I am,' I said with a slow smile.

She looked at me for a long moment, then her lips lifted again in an even wider grin. 'My name's Cheyenne.'

The memory of that meeting fuels my determination, and I give Adanna a hard stare. 'Are you going to rat me out?'

Adanna grimaces but holds my gaze. 'No.' Relieved, I push off the bed, but she isn't finished. 'I'm coming too.'

I shake my head. *No way!*

'And the best part is that you actually can't stop me,' Adanna points out with a grim smirk.

A dozen thoughts run through my head, including tying her up, but the determination on her face stops them. I should fight harder. I don't want to put Adanna in danger, and my parents are going to freak out when they realize, but I can't make myself say the words. I don't want to do this on my own.

'Fine.' I begin to pace across the floor. 'Dr Dòyìnbó must be keeping Cheyenne at the academy. He was in his office in the video call.' I stop in front of my bed. 'If we can sneak in, maybe we can sneak Chey out.'

Adanna shakes her head. 'DAMI has that place locked tight. You can't just sneak into AOS undetected.'

'Zahrah and some of the other Òmìnira got in that time after Ìdánwò,' I point out.

'True, but their inside spy must have helped them. And even so, we found Zahrah pretty quickly. Remember how the emergency alarm went off,' Adanna reminds me. 'DAMI is programmed to send a school-wide alert whenever there's an unauthorized security breach.'

My heart sinks. If we can't get into the academy, we're stuck.

Beside me, Adanna's breathing speeds up suddenly. 'But maybe we can use that to our benefit?' I frown at her, not understanding. 'DAMI instructs everyone to go to their rooms when the emergency alarm sounds, right?' she continues, seeing my confusion.

'Yeah, so what?'

'If everyone is safe in their rooms, then they won't catch us looking for Chey.'

'Okay. But what happens when they figure out there's no emergency?' I query.

'I'll have to lock them in their rooms,' says Adanna in a reluctant voice.

'You can do that?'

'I can control DAMI.' She grins.

My eyes swing to her. 'Huh?'

She shrugs. 'I've always been able to.' My eyebrows lift, and she shakes her head in warning. 'It was too painful before because of how much Ike it uses. I can't do it for very long either.'

'You never told me that!'

Adanna shrugs. 'Dr Dòyìnbó made me keep it a secret. He thought it would make the other Solari uncomfortable.'

'So you're saying we can use Dr Dòyìnbó's own system against him and no one will get hurt?'

'It still feels wrong to lock the others up,' Adanna mumbles.

I reach for her hand and squeeze it. 'Please, Ada,' I plead. 'It's not for long and it's our only option.'

Irritation flares in her eyes and she pulls away. 'We could also just wait like your dad said and do this as a team.'

I swallow as a churning begins in my stomach. I need this to work. I need Adanna. Then an idea hits me.

'I guess I could just knock on the front door instead,' I say. 'Then you could sneak in while Big Head chases me around the campus.'

Adanna rolls her eyes. 'You're being ridiculous and I'm not falling for it.'

I start jogging around the room, pretending I'm being chased. Then, with a loud groan, Adanna picks up a nearby pillow and throws it at me. I dodge it easily.

'Fine!' she huffs. 'For the record, I hate you and this plan. It's ridiculous.'

I return to my bed and throw my arms round her. 'Thank you!'

Adanna pushes me away, but not before I see the concerned frown she quickly hides. 'Don't thank me yet. We still have to find Chey in that maze of a place. Dr Dòyìnbó could be hiding her anywhere. I can probably keep us hidden from the security system, but . . .' The frown returns.

'What?' I ask.

'If Dr Dòyìnbó figures out our plan, all he has to do is reboot and disable DAMI. I'll lose access and this whole plan falls apart.'

'We'll just have to be quick then,' I say in a determined voice.

'There's no turning back if we do this.' Adanna's voice is gentle, but it doesn't make her words sound any less scary.

We're really doing this.

'I'm going to have to encrypt all the access channels,' Adanna adds, her voice suddenly distracted. 'I'll have to bypass DAMI's primary protocols though . . .'

She starts to spout a load of techy stuff and I stop listening. This is the first time I'm disobeying Papa and, for some reason, the thought makes the craziness of our plan feel so much more real. I try not to think about how my parents, aunt, or the rest of Nchebe will react once they find out. Hopefully they won't be too angry once we're back with Cheyenne. I hold on to that thought. It's the only one that really matters anyway.

Hold on, Chey! I'm coming.

'There's still one problem,' Adanna says, forcing my attention back to her.

'What?'

'How do we get to AOS?'

CHAPTER TWENTY-FOUR

The Hyperloop is all sleek metal and glass as it soars above the Lagos skyline. Each pod is made up of two rows of leather seats with enough space for four people. My seat has its own screen with a virtual map of Lagos flashing across it. I even have a cup holder. I never imagined my first time using the Hyperloop would be because I was sneaking away from my parents so I could break into the Academy of the Sun.

The scarf wrapped round my hair is too tight, and I run a finger along the edge, trying to ease the pressure. Before we'd left the safe house, Adanna had given it to me.

'We need to blend in,' she'd insisted.

I'd stared at it blankly, something inside me bristling at the thought of wearing it. It's been a while since I felt like I needed to hide my hair, but then Adanna pushed a baseball cap over her own, so I nodded and took the scarf, stuffing as much of my hair into it as possible.

Sneaking out of the safe house was a lot easier than I'd thought it would be. Everyone was so distracted by Dr Dòyìnbó's call and planning our escape that no one paid much attention to me and Adanna. There was a moment, just as we were about to leave through the back entrance, that I thought Zahrah had spotted us. But then she turned away and we quickly darted out.

Now we're in the Hyperloop cabin, I understand why Adanna was so insistent on me covering my hair. There are cameras everywhere, and my hair was made to stand out.

Adanna and I get off at Ebute-Metta station, which is the closest station to the academy and only about fifteen minutes from the safe house in the super-fast pod. The walk to the outer edges of the campus takes us another twenty minutes. I've never entered the academy from the ground, and it takes me a moment to get my bearings. We arrive at an enormous set of iron gates. Two imposing solid panels of metal stamped with the school crest stand between us and Cheyenne. Above the gates, a black metal dome glares down, the glass eye of the camera lens fixed on us.

'Ada—' I begin, shooting her a worried glance. But Adanna's not looking at me; her eyes are closed. My voice skitters to a stop.

'Don't move,' Adanna whispers, just as a beam of blue light shoots out from the dome, passing over us like a scanner.

A look of concentration passes over her face, like it does whenever she uses her technopath Ike. The beam continues for a few more seconds and I barely let myself breathe. Then, just as suddenly as it started, the beam stops and the gates swing open in a wide arc. Adanna doesn't pause, striding through, and I scuttle after her. We follow the driveway a short distance until we arrive at a security checkpoint, but it's empty. There's no sign of the guards that are supposed to patrol campus.

Then I spot a boy in an academy uniform, and I crash to a halt. *Where did he come from?* It feels weird seeing the patterned shorts and blue polo shirt of House Psionic again. But there's something not quite right about him. The skin on his face is super smooth ... impossibly so. The boy's thick lips lift in a welcoming and far-too-perfect-looking smile.

'Welcome back, Adanna,' he says.

The deep metallic voice sounds familiar, but I struggle to place it. Then it clicks.

'DAMI?' I gasp.

His smile grows even wider. 'I'm an avatar of DAMI. How can I help?'

My own smile is shaky. Adanna never said DAMI could do this, though I guess it makes sense given the level of tech at the academy.

'We don't have much time,' Adanna says. 'Activate protocol ADA24.'

'One moment, please.' The avatar's eyes flash up into its head for a second, and I wince. 'Protocol ADA24 initiated.'

'How long will it take for everyone to make their way to their rooms?' Adanna asks the avatar.

'It took approximately fifteen minutes during the last practice drill.'

'What about the guards?' I ask, looking around at the deserted campus. 'Where is everyone?'

'All non-essential staff were dismissed by Dr Dòyìnbó a week ago,' the avatar responds.

So that explains why we haven't met any resistance so far. *But why?*

Adanna shakes her head as if reading my mind. 'That's not a good sign. He must be trying to isolate the Solari.'

The fifteen-minute wait feels like for ever, but finally DAMI's eyes flash again.

'Protocol ADA24 complete,' the avatar says in a steady voice.

'Lock it down,' Adanna commands.

'Are you certain?' DAMI replies. 'All rooms except common areas will be locked indefinitely.'

Indecision flashes over Adanna's face. Then she straightens. 'Do it.'

The avatar blinks. 'Lockdown protocol complete.'

'Thanks, DAMI,' Adanna says. 'Now go into hibernation mode.'

The avatar's eyes flash one last time before he suddenly disappears, like a genie called back into its lamp.

'Come on,' says Adanna as she shoots off towards the quad.

She moves along one of the hibiscus-lined paths silently. I scramble after her, not nearly as quiet. I scan the quad, looking for any signs of other Solari, but there's no movement anywhere. A shiver skates down my back as I remember what's at stake if we mess this up.

I glance towards Adanna, but she's still way ahead of me. Then the main building appears. Staying low, she approaches the glass doors and they part smoothly. She steps through and, after a moment, turns back and motions for me to follow.

We don't linger, moving quickly past the huge baobab tree growing in the middle of the atrium. Past the big screen of rankings that proclaims Ẹni as the new leader. Past the classrooms where I studied alongside my fellow Solari. We continue through the familiar hallways and towards Dr Dòyìnbó's office. We decided to start there, hoping we might find a clue as to where Cheyenne's being kept. We've yet to see anyone, but I can't help worrying. Just like at the lodge in Old Oyo National Park, this feels way too easy.

'Can you dial it down?' says Adanna. 'I can smell you freaking out and I need to concentrate.'

'I don't like this, Ada. Something feels off,' I say, my voice low and urgent.

210

'We don't have time for worrying,' Adanna replies. 'We have a job to do, so let's get on with it and get out of here.'

Soon we're outside Dr Dòyìnbó's office and I tense. *He's locked in his room*, I remind myself. Then Adanna lifts the holomorpher out of her pocket, and I frown, unsure what she's doing. She wouldn't tell me anything about this part. She said the less I knew, the better. She waves the wand-like device over her face, and her features begin to wobble. I step back in amazement as her face morphs into Dr Dòyìnbó's, right down to the laughter lines around his eyes. My heart begins to race, and I step back. *It's not him … It's not him*, I remind myself.

'I finally perfected it.' The voice is Adanna's and the weirdness of it is proper disturbing. I shudder, but she just winks at me before turning back to the door. She places her face near a darkened panel. The panel lights up, then, with a soft click, the door swings open. Adanna smirks at me with her borrowed face.

'That's just wrong,' I tell her.

Adanna blinks three times in quick succession and Dr Dòyìnbó's face melts away, replaced by hers, right down to her dimples.

Adanna flashes them at me. 'Better?' I nod. 'Oya, let's go,' she commands, before stepping through the open door. I follow slowly, suddenly nervous again.

'I'm going to check the computer,' says Adanna, moving to Dr Dòyìnbó's desk. 'Look for anything that seems out of place.'

211

I nod and turn away, scanning for clues. The room is perfectly tidy as usual, right down to the stuffed bookshelf that spans the wall opposite the desk. Everything looks normal though. I turn back to Adanna, but her attention is totally focused on the computer in front of her.

'Did you find something?' I ask.

Adanna nods. 'Dr Dòyìnbó's got everyone convinced we're spies.' Her eyes continue to scan the glass screen. 'Even the Councils. I was right. If we'd approached them, we'd have been arrested immediately.'

She goes silent, distracted by whatever she's reading, so I go back to searching the room. Then something odd catches my attention. Six picture frames line the far wall. In each is a photograph of one of Nigeria's past leaders, right up to the current one. Each Laamu-EzeOba is arranged in chronological order ... except the second and the third are the wrong way round.

Have they always been like that?

Orji Tobechukwu should be second. I remember from one of Professor Sàlàkọ́'s history lessons that it was under his leadership that Dr Dòyìnbó discovered trarium and the country moved to solar power. It seems a strange mistake for Dr Dòyìnbó to make. I think back to what Adanna said about looking for anything out of place.

'I think I've found something.'

Adanna glances at me, a look of irritation on her face. She

really hates being interrupted when she's reading. I roll my eyes and wave her over. Together, we lift the photograph from the wall. My fingers tingle in anticipation, and it only increases when I see what's behind the portrait. The small keypad embedded in the wall is totally not what I was expecting.

'Looks like we need a code,' Adanna whispers.

'What do you think it is?'

There's a short silence before she speaks. 'I have no idea.'

My stomach sinks and I stare at the keypad in frustration. Then an idea hits me.

'Try 1975.' Adanna gives me a funny look. 'It's the year Orji Tobechukwu became Laamu-EzeOba,' I insist.

Adanna shrugs but enters the numbers. The pad beeps its acceptance and I grin triumphantly. *I guess Professor Sàlàkọ́'s history lessons do have their uses.* Then the bookcase next to us begins to rumble and my jaw drops.

'No way!' I breathe.

Adanna stares at me, frozen in place, as what we thought was merely a bookcase springs open like a secret trapdoor.

'Wow!' Adanna gasps. 'How did Dr Dòyìnbó have a secret hideout in here and I had no idea about it?'

I grin at her disgruntled expression. Adanna's spent so much time in here looking through Dr Dòyìnbó's research books that I'm kind of surprised she's never found it either. I quickly head for the door, pulling it wider to find a darkened tunnel beyond. The grey concrete walls stretch ahead, a faint glow of light pulsing from somewhere further down. *Could Cheyenne be somewhere in here?* If I was Dr Dòyìnbó, this is where I'd hide someone. My feet are moving before I can stop them.

I step into the corridor, keeping Ike on high alert just in case. The sound of Adanna's breathing is loud behind me, but I ignore it, focusing instead on the beam of light ahead. We move in silence, pushing deeper into the narrow corridor. The faint glow of light shimmers and we continue towards it, finally reaching an open doorway. The light winks enticingly at us.

I look at Adanna and she shrugs, so I draw a deep breath and step through. It takes a moment for my eyes to adjust to the sudden light, then the details of the stark space become clearer. Bright white walls reflect off a gleaming tiled floor, and metal pipes cross-cross the ceiling. In front of me are two smaller rooms sealed behind glass doors that stretch from one wall to another like prison cells.

The one closest to me is occupied by a familiar man lying on a single bed with his head bowed and his eyes closed ... *It's Bukola!*

My stomach tightens at the sight of the Òmìnira, and I rush towards the locked door. But there's no handle, nor any locking system. Frustrated, I strike the glass hard with my closed fist. Bukola's eyes blink open, his head turning towards me with a confused frown on his face. Our eyes meet, but there's no sign of recognition from him. It's almost as if he doesn't know I'm there. Then realization hits me.

'He can't see us,' I breathe.

'It must be a two-way mirror,' Adanna says, coming up behind me. 'He probably can't see out from his side.'

'Stand back,' I instruct, before calling up Ike.

I send a thick bolt of hair at the glass and brace for the shattering impact. But it doesn't come. Instead, my hair hits the glass with a loud thud before bouncing back harmlessly. Bukola jumps back in shock on the other side.

Adanna looks at me with a surprise I share. *The glass must be bulletproof.* After a moment, Bukola moves close to the glass again, his right hand reaching out to rest against it. I place my left hand against his, the cold of the surface seeping into me. Fresh anger wells up inside me. *Dr Dòyìnbó has to be stopped!*

I switch my attention to the other cell, identical to the first, only this one is open. Before I can wonder why, I spy a girl sleeping on a narrow bed resting against a wall. Her back is to me, but I'd know those cosplay fox ears anywhere.

'Cheyenne!' I cry.

I rush into the cell and reach Cheyenne in seconds, dropping down beside her. The smell of coconut oil hits me immediately.

'Onyeka?' Adanna calls sharply as she follows me.

But I'm beyond listening, my focus fixed on my best friend. Her eyes are closed, and one of the reddish-brown fox ears is wonky. I shake her shoulder and she stirs, then her dark eyes open.

'Hey,' I whisper. 'It's Super Yeka.'

Cheyenne's eyes widen in recognition, and she bolts upright. 'You shouldn't be in here,' she says urgently. 'It's not safe—'

But her words are lost beneath the scraping sound that comes from the entrance to the cell behind me. I turn to see the door closing, and a harsh shout leaves me. I call my Ike instinctively and a bolt of hair rushes towards the door, flying past a startled Adanna. But I'm too late.

'What the . . . ?' Adanna begins.

The sound of the door slamming shut cuts her off. I stand and rush towards it, searching for a handle, but there isn't one on this side either. My panicked reflection stares back at me. Adanna stands next to me now, pounding on the mirrored glass that has us trapped.

'Can't you open it?' I ask her.

Adanna shakes her head. 'The lock isn't electronic. Nothing in this room is.'

I stare at her as I realize what that means. *Dr Dòyìnbó was expecting us.*

'Welcome back, Onyeka. I knew you'd come.'

The voice that fills the room is deep and amused. I swivel round, looking for Dr Dòyìnbó, but there's no one here except us.

'Where are you?' I demand, my voice harsh.

'All will be revealed soon,' comes the knowing reply. 'For now, you might want to make yourself comfortable.'

My body sags and my legs feel like jelly. *What have I done?*

CHAPTER
TWENTY-FIVE

I straighten up slowly and turn to find Cheyenne still on the bed, studying us.

'Are you okay?' I ask her.

Cheyenne rubs her eyes sleepily. 'It depends.'

I make my way back over to her. 'On what?'

She adjusts her fox ears before speaking. 'On whether this is all part of your master plan and the rest of your Solari friends are going to show up any minute.' I look away. 'I knew it!' Cheyenne exclaims, then she looks at Adanna. 'I expect this from her.' Her finger waves at me accusingly. 'But what's your excuse?'

Adanna's grunt is quiet, though the stomp of her feet as she moves away from the door is proper loud, so is the scowl on her face.

'It's not her fault,' I say quickly. 'I didn't give her a choice. I wanted to get you out of here so badly.'

'Of course you did,' Cheyenne replies with a sniff. 'But it would have been better to do it successfully, yeah?'

I suppress the urge to kick her. Trust Cheyenne to give me major attitude even when we're in a whole heap of trouble.

'DAMI?' Adanna calls, finally speaking. But there's no reply, only eerie silence. 'They must have rebooted him.' Her eyes snap to me, then flick away just as quickly. 'Like I said they would.'

'Just say it,' I say with a sigh, but Adanna shakes her head. 'You know you want to.'

A mutinous expression settles over her face, and Cheyenne stares between us curiously.

'What's going on?'

I point at Adanna. 'She's angry because she warned me this would happen.'

'I'M NOT ANGRY!' Adanna's screech cuts across my words, sending my ears ringing. Her body begins to shake, and I brace myself. *She's going to finish me.* Yet, when she does speak, her voice is surprisingly calm. 'Are you happy now?' I stiffen at her words. 'You wanted to go off and save the day on your own, so are you happy now?' Adanna repeats.

'It's not like I meant for any of this to happen. I was just trying to help Chey,' I finally reply. It's a feeble effort though, and we both know it.

Adanna plants her hands on her hips, staring me down. 'Not good enough. You've been acting really off ever since we found out about Dr Dòyìnbó's true intentions. I've tried to be understanding and not push back.'

'I know,' I say through gritted teeth. A spark of power pulses through me, and my eyes flash a warning. 'I'm sorry, okay?'

Adanna shakes her head sadly. 'You still don't get it, do you?'

'Get what?'

'Because of us, Dr Dòyìnbó is definitely going to get his hands on the serum now. Your parents won't have a choice.' I look at her properly, finally seeing the thin trail of tears sliding down her cheeks. She roughly wipes them away. 'We've practically handed it over with a big fat bow.'

'I didn't know it was a trap,' I whisper. My throat feels scratchy. 'I couldn't sit about doing nothing.'

'I—I—I,' Adanna exclaims. 'This isn't just about you. You keep making decisions like it only affects you. I know you're hurting, but you're not the only one Dr Dòyìnbó betrayed. He betrayed *all* of us. But you've been too busy pushing everyone away to notice how the rest of us feel.'

Her words strike a nerve, and I suck in a sharp breath. My eyes lower, unable to meet her gaze. She's right. I've built a wall of fear and guilt around me. I thought it would protect me from getting hurt again, but it's only made everything worse. I can't hide from my emotions like I used to, and I don't know how to manage the negative ones that have been driving me, eating away at my ability to think beyond my feelings. Dr Dòyìnbó took something other than my parents from me – he took away my trust. Now I don't know who or what to believe any more.

Pressure builds inside my chest until I feel like I'll never be able to breathe again. I clutch my arms, trying to hold myself together as a tear slides down my own cheek.

'I'm so worried and scared all the time.' The full truth finally bursts from me in a broken sob. 'I thought if I kept moving, the horrible feelings would pass and no one would notice there was something wrong.'

Cheyenne steps between us, and Adanna turns away, dropping down on the bed.

'I remember how you used to count using the Fibonacci sequence to control your emotions,' Cheyenne says slowly, like she's trying to find the right words. 'I used to watch you, wondering what it must be like to never let yourself feel anything. To always be running from yourself. It's why I was so happy when I found out about Ike and the Solari, because it meant that you had to finally deal with your feelings.'

A snort leaves me. 'I'm doing a great job of that, aren't I?'

'You just like being extra,' Cheyenne says with a grin. 'You don't have to take on *all* the feelings at the same time, you know.'

I frown at her. 'I'm not.'

Cheyenne gives me an epic side-eye, then her expression turns rueful. 'When you left London, I was mopey for ages. I drove the 'rents bonkers. Mum even threatened to take away my fox ears if I didn't fix up.' I gape at her. Things must have been proper serious for Cheyenne's mum to say that. 'Then Dad told me it was okay to be sad and even a bit angry about losing you. But he also reminded me about how much of an amazing opportunity going to Nigeria was for you and your mum. He said he'd noticed your confidence growing whenever we video-called.'

'You were angry?' I ask. This is news to me. *Why didn't Cheyenne tell me?*

'You're getting distracted,' Cheyenne says. 'The point I'm trying to make is that feelings are cool and everything, but you can't let the negative ones take over, because they don't let you see everything clearly, especially the good stuff.' Cheyenne shrugs. 'At least, I think that's what Dad was trying to say.'

Her words make a confusing sort of sense. I *have* let my negative emotions block out everything else that's been going on. Yes, things have been difficult, but I've had Nchebe and my aunt with me. Plus, we found my parents and the Òmìnira. Even in the darkest moments, there's always been hope, love and even laughter.

How did I lose sight of that? Why did I let my fear and guilt drive my decisions? Maybe it's because I haven't had much practice working through my feelings. I've spent so many years running from and supressing them by using the Fibonacci numbers. I stare at Cheyenne, slightly impressed.

'When did you get so smart?'

Cheyenne gives me a gentle shove. 'Shut up. I'm practically a guru. I've even started doing yoga.'

I wipe my cheek. 'If you're such a genius, how do I manage all these feelings then?'

'You could try not being so hard on yourself,' Adanna pipes up from her corner. 'You're powerful, but you're not perfect, and no one needs you to be. But you do need to let us in so we can help you.'

Be kind to yourself ... You don't have to be perfect ... Let people in.

The words slam into my mind, burrowing deep until they're spinning round and round like a whirlwind. They're so simple, yet so powerful, and something loosens inside me. I'm suddenly cold, and a shiver wracks my body. It turns into a shaking I can't seem to stop. Then more tears come as a great big jerking sob escapes my mouth.

Cheyenne moves first and her arms close round me. I stiffen, but she doesn't let go. Her arms tighten even further like a fence, holding me together and at the same time keeping out the pain and hurt. I burrow my head into her shoulder, letting the warmth from her seep into me. Then another set of arms joins Cheyenne's. I look up, my eyes meeting Adanna's, and the understanding blazing from them. We stay like that for a long moment.

'You're squishing me!'

Cheyenne's muffled protest breaks the moment and suddenly

we're all laughing. It feels easy and good, and I never want it to end. But I don't have that luxury. We still have to get out of here.

'So, what happened to you?' Adanna asks Cheyenne, letting the both of us go before standing up. 'How did you manage to get yourself kidnapped?'

Cheyenne rolls her eyes and gets up too. 'I didn't exactly invite Dr Dòyìnbó to Birmingham, you know. I was minding my business at art camp.'

'How was it?' I ask curiously.

'Amazing,' Cheyenne squeals. 'I'm going to kick Dr Dòyìnbó's butt for making me miss it.'

Adanna clears her throat. 'Erm, can we focus, please?'

'Sorry,' Cheyenne replies sheepishly. 'I decided to get to the art studio early one morning so I could nab the best position.'

'Near a big window, right?' I know how particular Cheyenne is about her environment when she's drawing.

'Fam! You can't beat natural light.' Adanna groans loudly, and Cheyenne throws her a sheepish look. 'It was still really early, and I was alone, walking from my dorm to the art studio. Then a strange girl in a violet headtie approached me, saying you were in trouble and that we had to leave immediately.

'Ẹni,' Adanna says with a grimace.

'She knew all about you and the Solari, so I followed her to this epic-looking plane that was super-fast. By the time we arrived at the academy, I realized something was wrong, but it

223

was too late.' Cheyenne rubs one of her furry ears. 'My parents must be freaking out.'

I quickly explain about the fake message Dr Dòyìnbó left, and Cheyenne calms a little.

'How long ago did this happen?' I ask.

'I don't know, maybe a day or two? It's kind of hard to tell in here.'

Adanna frowns. 'Have you seen anyone else?'

Cheyenne pulls a face. 'A boy with really dark eyes.'

Adanna and I share a glance.

'Òré,' I say.

Cheyenne gives us a perplexed look. 'Okaaaaay ... He and the girl have been bringing my meals. The boy's nice – he keeps asking if I'm okay – and the food isn't too bad, actually.' Then her mouth turns down a little. 'No akara though. I swear the girl keeps taking bites out of my food too.'

'Definitely Ẹni,' Adanna says with a knowing look.

I resist the urge to smile at Cheyenne's annoyed tone. At least Dr Dòyìnbó's been feeding her. I look around the room, studying every inch of it. Metal pipes run across the ceiling with fluorescent lights shining from them. There aren't any windows or vents, and our only exit is still very much locked. And thanks to me, no one else knows where we are.

Stop! I quickly shut that last thought down. *I will not feed the negative thoughts.*

'We need to figure out a way to get out of here,' I say aloud.

'Now you're talking,' Cheyenne replies. 'We can't let Dr Dòyìnbó play us like this.'

Adanna looks at the locked door thoughtfully. 'You said that Eni and Òrẹ́ have been bringing your meals?' Cheyenne nods. 'That's our chance. When the next meal arrives, we'll make a run for it. Between Onyeka and I, we should be able to deal with whoever turns up.'

I nod, and the three of us share a determined look. It's as good a plan as any. I hope Òrẹ́ comes first. Maybe we can talk some sense into him.

'I really hope it's Eni,' Cheyenne says, an evil look on her face.

A few hours later and we're still waiting for someone to turn up. Every squeak, creak or thud has us rushing to get into position, only to be disappointed.

'This is getting boring,' Cheyenne says, flopping down onto the bed. Then we hear another creak. Cheyenne groans, but Adanna stiffens.

'Shhh,' she whispers. 'Someone is definitely coming. I can hear their eagerness.'

I quickly move into position again, hooking a bolt of hair round one of the metal pipes above me. I power up my Ike and lift myself up so I'm suspended directly above the door. The plan is for Adanna to distract whoever comes through long enough for me to surprise them from above. Within moments, the mirrored door swings open, and a boy walks through. Adanna moves to intercept him, but then she stops suddenly, her whole body freezing in place.

'Wait,' Adanna cries, but it's too late.

My hair whips out, wrapping itself round the boy.

'Abeg o, make you put me for ground.'

'Hassan?' I gasp and quickly release him.

I drop down, landing in front of him and Adanna. But he isn't alone. Niyì and Zahrah enter the cell too. Then Papa appears, followed by Ọ̀rẹ́ and Professor Sàlàkọ́. I don't have time to wonder why those two are here because my father zeroes in on me. His face is frozen in a hard expression, and I suck in a sharp breath, waiting for the epic telling off that's coming my way.

Papa reaches me in three strides, and I tense. Then his big arms surround me, lifting me clear off the ground and into a tight hug I wasn't expecting.

'Thank God we found you,' Papa whispers into my hair.

CHAPTER
TWENTY-SIX

'What are you doing here?' I gasp.

Papa pulls away, just enough to give me a stern look. 'Shouldn't I be asking you that, young lady? Your mother is frantic with worry.'

I swallow hard. I hadn't let myself think too hard about how my parents would feel after I disappeared.

'I'm sorry,' I say quietly. 'Where *is* Mum?'

'With your aunt at a new safe house.'

'You should have seen her,' Niyì says in awe. 'She was ready to take on Dr Dòyìnbó with just her fists. But your dad wouldn't let her come.'

My dad grimaces and I give him a sympathetic smile. I can totally see it. Mum can be proper scary when she's in the mood. One time, when the local council refused to come fix a leak in our house back in London, Mum camped out in front of their office for two whole days.

'How did you find us though?' I press.

'You no wise,' Hassan replies with a hurt expression. 'Why you no wait for us?'

'Abeg, no vex,' I reply in Pidgin. I need him to know how sorry I am.

After a moment Hassan nods his acceptance of my apology. 'No wahala.'

My gaze switches to Niyì. 'No more lies or running off. I promise.'

Niyì shrugs. 'It's not like I haven't had my own issues.'

Zahrah steps forward then. 'After we discovered you were missing, I contacted my father and he suggested we use our spy in AOS to locate you.'

Their spy? That's when it clicks.

'Professor Sàlàkọ́?' I gasp.

I eye the professor's narrow frame with newfound respect. If I'd had to guess, I'd have gone for Ms Bello. She actually looks like a spy.

'Thank you for helping us find my dad,' I say.

Professor Sàlàkọ́ gives me a small bow, and behind him I spot Ọ̀rẹ́. He catches my gaze and shifts nervously. I understand why the professor is here, but that doesn't explain Ọ̀rẹ́. I glare at him. The last time I saw him, he was calling us traitors. And he helped Dr Dòyìnbó kidnap Cheyenne!

'What about him?' I growl, pointing in Ọ̀rẹ́'s direction.

Hassan raises his hands. 'Calm down o. Na Ọ̀rẹ́ help us find you.'

'So you believe us now?' I sneer.

'Yes,' Ọ̀rẹ́ says in a quiet voice. 'I found Adanna's encrypted message in our Scrabble game.' I look at Adanna and she grins.

'I embedded some of Dr Uduike's research into it,' Adanna says.

My dad startles. 'You did what?'

'It was the only thing I could think of. What if something happened to us? No one would ever know what Dr Dòyìnbó did. I couldn't let that happen.'

Dad's mouth softens. 'I understand, but it was still incredibly dangerous.'

Adanna gives him an *I'm not stupid* look. 'I didn't embed everything. Just enough to make Ọ̀rẹ́ start questioning things.'

'I didn't believe it at first,' Ọ̀rẹ́ says. 'But the more I looked into it, the more legit it became. It's been really strange at the academy since you guys left.'

'How so?' my dad asks.

'Dr Dòyìnbó put AOS into lockdown and all these soldiers showed up. Then we started having to do these odd military drills. Dr Dòyìnbó said it was to prepare us should we need to defend Nigeria, but he wouldn't tell us what from. There's also been a total social media blackout, so we haven't heard anything from the outside world. Professor Sàlàkọ́ is the only person that still feels normal.'

'Only AOSnet is accessible, and even that's been limited,' Professor Sàlàkọ́ adds.

Ọ̀rẹ́'s gaze slides to Cheyenne, but he quickly looks away again. 'Then Dr Dòyìnbó forced us to kidnap your friend. He said it was the only way to make you guys co-operate. But that doesn't make it right.'

Professor Sàlàkọ́ places a hand on Ọ̀rẹ́'s shoulder. 'Dr Dòyìnbó's been running a campaign of misinformation. Solari are being fed lies about the Councils having turned against the Nigerian people, and they have no way of verifying if it's true. Dr Dòyìnbó has also been interfering with students' dreams to try to influence them. Young Ọ̀rẹ́ came to me recently and revealed his worries, and I tried to reassure him without revealing too much of the truth. I warned Ọ̀gá Gbénga in my last communications with him that I believe Dr Dòyìnbó is preparing to take over the Councils, and soon.'

Ọ̀rẹ́ nods. 'After AOS went into lockdown, Professor Sàlàkọ́ found me and explained everything. It made complete sense. The soldiers, the dreams – it all adds up. Adanna's annoying, but she's no traitor, and even though I haven't known Onyeka for long, I didn't understand how the person who helped me and Chigozie during Ìdánwò could be a traitor or turn rogue like Dr Dòyìnbó was saying.'

I remember that moment weeks ago from the first trial of Ìdánwò when Chigozie nearly fell from a floating holographic rock. I'd gone back to help her, never imagining that my actions then would help us now.

'I knew you'd see sense.' Adanna nudges his arm with her elbow. 'Took you long enough though.'

Òrẹ́ gives her a strained smile. 'I told Professor Sàlàkọ́ where to find you guys. I refuse to be used as a weapon.'

Òrẹ́ has been very helpful,' the professor confirms. 'Once I had your location, I contacted Ọ̀gá Gbénga.'

'We came as soon as my father told us,' Zahrah adds.

Professor Sàlàkọ́ looks behind him nervously. 'We don't have much time. I was able to smuggle your rescue party in only because Dr Dòyìnbó called a whole school meeting. Everyone is gathered in the main hall.'

I'd heard all about the main hall during the brief time I was at the academy. I never got to see it though as it's only used for formal events or major emergencies.

'Do you know why?' I ask, concern creeping into my voice.

Professor Sàlàkọ́ shakes his head. 'I suspect Dr Dòyìnbó is about to activate his plans to take over Nigeria. He was so certain your father would hand over the formula for the new serum, but without it, he knows he doesn't have time to waste. The Solari here are already agitated and unsure, but their faith in him is strong. If he tells them they must fight, they will.'

'We have to warn them,' Cheyenne cries.

I nod. 'We can't let the Solari go to war for Dr Dòyìnbó.'

'How are we supposed to stop him?' Zahrah says. 'We're outnumbered and in enemy territory.'

231

'They're not our enemies,' Niyì protests. 'They're Solari, just like us.'

Zahrah rolls her eyes. 'You know what I mean. They still have an advantage.'

'And we don't even have a plan,' Adanna adds.

'We have the truth,' I reply.

Zahrah snorts and stares at me like I'm nuts. 'What are you going to do? Go barging into a hall full of Solari and tell them their leader is a liar?'

I stare right back. 'If I have to, yes.'

My dad places a hand on my shoulder. 'Onyeka—' he begins in a warning voice, but I shrug him off.

'You know I'm right.' I turn to the others. 'We don't have time to wait any more. We have to tell everyone the truth, and we have to do it now.'

Zahrah looks doubtful. 'My father and the Òmìnira are on their way, but I don't know how long it will take them to get here. If we go in there now, we'll be entirely alone.'

'My friends will help,'   offers. 'I told Chigozie and a few others who I knew would believe me. They'll back us up.'

Silence floods the room as we look at each other. It's still not enough though, and we all know it. But this could be our only chance to stop Dr Dòyìnbó before it's too late.

'You'll only get one chance to convince everyone,' Niyì says.

Me? But they barely know me.

I open my mouth to remind him of this fact, but the determined look on Niyì's face stops me.

'This is your idea,' he declares. 'You should lead it.'

My eyes scan the faces of the people surrounding me. Cheyenne and Adanna give me a smile of encouragement and Hassan is practically grinning. There's a worried look on my dad's face, but there's also a fierce pride there too. Zahrah's face is its usual blank mask, but her clenched fist glows orange with a barely formed flame. *We have some unfinished business.* I step forward to face her.

'I'm sorry that my mistake led Dr Dòyìnbó to the Òmìnira compound and that I put your family in danger.' My voice is steady and so is my gaze as I hold hers. 'I've made a lot of stupid decisions lately, but that's over now.' I hold out a tentative hand. 'We work as a team, or not at all, so will you help me make this right?'

Zahrah's eyes flick to my hand then back to my face and I hold my breath, unsure what she's going to decide. Her red eyes drill into mine like laser beams searching for something. I don't flinch, hoping she can see how sincere I am. After a moment, she blinks, then holds out her fiery fist, a clear challenge blazing at me.

I don't hesitate, quickly clenching my hand to give her a slow fist bump. I wince at the contact, knowing I totally deserve the pain. A grudging smile breaks out on Zahrah's face as I pass her test. I take another look at my friends and family surrounding me. Now we're ready.

'Let's do this.'

CHAPTER TWENTY-SEVEN

We cross the distance between Dr Dòyìnbó's office and the main hall in silence. My father and I lead the way with Cheyenne at the rear accompanied by Ọ̀rẹ́. She's under strict instruction to stay put. I tried leaving her in the secret room, but she was having none of it. It was easier just to bring her along.

I've never felt so scared in my life. What we're planning to do is actually kind of crazy. *What if I fail? What if the Solari won't listen to us and Dr Dòyìnbó wins?* The crawling tendrils of these negative thoughts try to latch onto my fear, but I refuse to let them. I'm surrounded by my family and friends. I'm not alone . . . *I have help.*

A warm hand closes around mine and I look up at my dad. He squeezes my hand but says nothing.

The hallways are totally deserted, and as we approach the big metal doors of the main hall, it becomes clear that Dr

Dòyìnbó isn't taking any risks. Five guards are stationed outside the entrance, and when they spot us they straighten, aiming dangerous glares at us.

'Leave!'

My father's command is so soft, I'm probably the only one who heard him. Yet the soldiers freeze like startled deer. Then, without a word, they leave their positions and file past us like zombies. I give Papa an impressed look.

'We'll have the element of surprise,' he says when we reach the doors. 'It should buy you a few minutes, so use it wisely.'

I nod and step forward, but the doors don't open automatically the way they're supposed to. I turn to Adanna. Her eyes glaze over and the doors slide open, revealing a huge room full of people. Yellow light pours in through massive tinted solar glass windows on either side, and it bounces off the stark white walls that slope into an articulated ceiling covered in metal beams. There are banners everywhere and beneath them Dr Dòyìnbó's soldiers line the room, watching over row after row of seated Solari. They're grouped in their colour-coded houses, all the way to the front of the room where Dr Dòyìnbó stands on a stage behind a podium, dressed in his formal robes.

Every eye in the room swings towards us and whispered conversations break out. I swallow and my hands begin to tremble. All of the students are wearing Second Sight and there's a mixture of shock and confusion on the faces staring back at me. Dr Dòyìnbó doesn't look surprised though. He looks worried. *Good!*

'Stop them!' he yells, and immediately his soldiers converge on us.

But Nchebe is already moving, Zahrah right beside them.

'Go,' Niyì calls to me, a ball of solid ice already forming in his hand. 'We'll take care of them.'

Hassan nods his agreement before turning invisible so that I lose sight of him. The room erupts then as my friends work to keep me safe. One of Zahrah's fireballs whizzes past, and I force my legs to keep moving. Papa keeps pace with me and I'm grateful for his presence. Though, just like Aunt Naomi, he won't be able to use Ike again for a while.

We pass some of the seated Solari, and one of the soldiers gets too close. Before I can react, he goes sprawling to the ground. I look up to find Chigozie, her leg sticking out from her position at the end of the row. She gives me a smile before standing and joining the action. She's not the only one. Other Solari from the academy join the fight. They must be the rest of Òré's friends. The majority stay seated though, watching the action in confusion.

I keep my gaze on Dr Dòyìnbó's face as we get closer and see the expression of alarm growing. Satisfaction fills me. But I'm so busy enjoying it that I almost miss the arm that comes out of nowhere. I duck just in time, spinning to face Ẹni and the sneer across her face. I frown. I really don't need this right now. Before I can do anything, Adanna is beside me.

'I've got this.'

I don't argue, sidestepping them both as they begin circling each other. Each step up to the stage feels like a small mountain, and I climb slowly. Then Papa moves in front of me, stretching out to his full height and looking all sorts of impressive. Dr Dòyìnbó must be spooked because he reaches into his pocket and pulls out a thin laser knife. The red-hot blade flashes on as Dr Dòyìnbó lunges forward, but Papa easily sidesteps him and knocks the knife out of his hand. Without his soldiers to protect him, Dr Dòyìnbó scuttles away from the podium like a scared rabbit. He doesn't get far as Papa quickly restrains him.

Then Papa nods at me encouragingly, and I take Dr Dòyìnbó's place to face my fellow Solari. The remaining guards have already been subdued by my friends, and a sea of childish faces stare back at me expectantly. Some of them wear curious expressions, and others are so full of anger and mistrust that I want to run off the stage. But I can't . . . I won't.

'M-my name is Onyeka,' I begin, but my throat feels dry and my voice cracks. I take a deep breath and try again. 'You've been told that my friends and I are traitors and that we've turned rogue, but Dr Dòyìnbó has been lying to all of you. About us, about the Councils . . . even about the sickness we suffer from whenever we use Ike. He is, in fact, Solari too.'

There is a collective gasp of surprise at this final revelation.

'Are you really going to listen to them?' Dr Dòyìnbó bursts out. 'They're traitors. They've betrayed you and they've

237

betrayed their country. They even brought a Rogue spy in here to attack you.'

A low sound of murmured whispers spreads through the room as hostile and suspicious eyes turn to examine Zahrah. We've been taught to fear and hate Òmìnira for too long. Niyì and Hassan tighten protectively around her, but she's not bothered. Her red eyes blaze back, a challenge no one has the guts to answer.

'That's not true. Zahrah is our friend,' I say quickly. 'They aren't Rogues; they're Òmìnira. And they helped us after Dr Dòyìnbó betrayed us. Òmìnira aren't trying to destroy us. They've been trying to tell us the truth. Dr Dòyìnbó hasn't been training us to protect Nigeria. He wants to use us as his own personal army so he can take over the country.'

Dr Dòyìnbó struggles helplessly in my father's arms. 'You know me. Does that sound like something I would do?'

'Shut up,' my father growls, tightening his hold.

But it makes no difference. I can see from their faces that the Solari don't believe me. Just as I feared, these kids barely know me and have no reason to trust anything I have to say. Niyì should have done this. My eyes find him in the crowd. *Help me*, I plead silently.

'We can prove Dr Dòyìnbó has been lying,' Niyì says loudly. 'Use your thermal scanners and see for yourself who he truly is.'

Of course! Solari have a higher core body temperature than regular humans, and the thermal scanner in Second Sight can pick it up. It doesn't take long before the shouts and gasps begin. I know exactly what they're seeing – Dr Dòyìnbó lit up like a purple glow stick as Second Sight reveals his true nature. I search the faces of the Solari again and find a new uncertainty, a realization that if Dr Dòyìnbó has lied about this, he could lie about anything.

Ẹni shakes free of Adanna's hold and presses a hand to her chest. 'What's going on?' Her voice cracks on the last word.

Suddenly, Dr Dòyìnbó breaks out of my father's arms and runs to the front of the stage, his hands lifted in a battle call.

'Who do you serve?' he screams. It's the desperate sound of a man with nothing to lose.

I close my eyes, dreading the response.

'Nigeria!' comes the answering cry.

Then my eyes fly open again. It wasn't as loud as I expected, or as loud as it could be. The Solari are starting to believe us, and I see the exact moment Dr Dòyìnbó realizes this too.

'Defend your country,' he roars, spittle flying from his mouth.

'No,' I cry, but it's too late.

Solari are already moving, and I can almost taste the power in the air as Ike ignites. Fighting breaks out again as some of the academy Solari face off against my friends. Fa'idah, a JSS1 student from house Enhancer, grows to a massive size, but I can't tell which side she's on as she dives forward, her huge fists flying. Muhammad, one of the littles from the primary years, teleports out of the way of an oncoming energy blast.

He reappears on the other side of the room and rams his hover wheelchair into one of Fọlákúnlé's dupes. My jaw drops as Ẹni, of all people, wraps her stretchy body round another of his dupes. *I guess she's starting to believe us.*

Suddenly, a Solari lunges straight at me from my left ... Tósìn! He's the boy from my dreams. But before he can make contact, Ọ̀rẹ́ crashes into him in mid-air, pushing Tósìn away from me. They struggle on the ground, before rolling out of view. Other bodies clash against one another as Solari fight a war they don't even understand.

I feel sick as I watch the chaos erupting around me. This wasn't supposed to happen, but I don't know how to stop it. Dr Dòyìnbó turns to me, a horrible look of satisfaction stamped across his face.

'You cannot beat me,' he growls, just as Amandi, a JSS1 student with a supersonic voice, jumps on stage.

He opens his mouth and roars at me. I press my hands to my ears, trying to block it out, but the sound is like a solid wave, and it hits me hard, pushing me to the ground. I can barely think or move beyond the pain. Then Amandi stops, eyeing me grimly.

'Onyeka!' yells Papa. I try to answer him, but Amandi bellows again, the power of it pinning me in place. My voice is lost under the force of Amandi's, and I stare at Papa helplessly. He tries to yell something, but the sound fails to reach me.

'Hold on, I'm coming.'

Before I can respond, a long brown hand reaches out from

somewhere behind Amandi. His eyes widen as it gives him a wave before stretching impossibly towards him. In a flash, the hand is wrapped round his face, covering his mouth. The wall of sound cuts off immediately, and the force holding me in place fades away. Then the rest of Ẹni's body stretches forward to meet her arm. She smiles, just as a blast of energy hits her, knocking both her and Amandi off the stage.

Papa reaches me, an anxious look on his face. 'Are you okay?'

I nod as he helps me to my feet. *But where's Dr Dòyìnbó?*

I spot him trying to make a run for it. His body is crouched low as he weaves his way between the distracted bodies. *He's getting away again!* I reach for Ike and it responds as my hair swings out and wraps round his leg. Dr Dòyìnbó yelps as I lift him up, ready to pull him back onto the stage.

But then Dr Dòyìnbó's arm lashes out and something orange flashes before he drops back to the ground in a tumbling heap. A shower of dark strands follow him as my hair retracts. There's a strange tingling in my scalp, and I look back over to Dr Dòyìnbó. He's standing now, and I see the laser knife in his right hand and a vicious smile on his face. It takes me a second to realize what he's done.

He cut my hair!

Fresh rage fills me that he would dare do such a thing, and my hair whips out again, quickly knocking the knife away. It's another reminder of all the pain Dr Dòyìnbó has caused, and I feel the need for revenge fighting to take over. For a moment

I think it will win and that I won't be able to stop the hurt and anger, but then I push it aside. This isn't about me, and I can't afford to lose focus. I pull back my strands, ignoring the damage. Suddenly, a booming sound thunders through the hall, followed by a massive gust of wind that sends me and everyone else in the room staggering.

What was that?

We all turn as one, following the powerful sound to the back of the hall, only to find Ọ̀gá Gbénga, flanked by Emem, Uche and dozens of the Òmìnira behind them. The fighting stops at once. We've never had so many strangers in AOS before, and no one knows who they are or what to do. I do though and my heart lifts. The Òmìnira are our chance to end this.

Before I can speak, Uche raises his arms wide then claps them together hard. The booming sound comes again, followed by another surge of energy that sends me to my knees and many others flying. *So this is his Ike.*

'Enough!' thunders Ọ̀gá Gbénga.

Then he and the Òmìnira sweep into the room and Zahrah joins her father, taking her place by his side. Their presence is electrifying, and I can almost feel the restless energy that follows them. Dr Dòyìnbó glares at Ọ̀gá Gbénga as he and Zahrah reach him near the front of the stage. Ọ̀gá Gbénga steps closer to Dr Dòyìnbó, getting right into his personal space.

'I'm back,' he declares in a harsh voice. 'And your time is up.'

CHAPTER TWENTY-EIGHT

'I knew you'd return one day, Gbénga,' Dr Dòyìnbó says in a soft voice.

Ọ̀gá Gbénga steps back with a frown. 'I'm not here for a reunion. I've contacted the Councils and sent them all of Benjamin's research. They'll be here soon to arrest you.'

Dr Dòyìnbó merely smirks. 'They can try, but my Solari will not allow it.'

Ọ̀gá Gbénga's head tilts as he considers his foe. 'You'd really let them defend you? Let them risk their lives for your worthless one?'

'Everything I've done in the past has been working towards this very moment,' Dr Dòyìnbó says without remorse. 'This will be my final gift to you all.'

Ọ̀gá Gbénga sucks in a harsh breath. 'You're not sorry for any of it, are you? Even if I couldn't sense it, your pride and satisfaction is written all over your face.'

Dr Dòyìnbó laughs. 'My plan is almost complete. I've won.'

'You've won nothing,' my dad growls.

Ọgá Gbénga shakes his head, a disbelieving look on his face. 'Even now, staring defeat in the face, you can't admit you're wrong and that you made a mistake.'

'Why would I apologize for protecting this nation?' Dr Dòyìnbó sneers. 'Does a lion seek permission to protect its pride? You think you've stopped me, but what about them?' He spreads his hands towards the Solari gathered below us. 'I made them what they are. They're mine, and they're unstoppable.'

Ọgá Gbénga's eyes scan the room, taking everything in. I know what he's seeing – a room full of confused kids. Some of them look like they want to tear Dr Dòyìnbó apart, but the rest would clearly still follow him. We're torn and divided. So full of the lies we've been fed that we no longer know what to believe and who to trust. I have no idea how to fix it, but I have to believe that we can undo the damage Dr Dòyìnbó has done to us.

'You're right,' Ọgá Gbénga finally says, and a look of anguish flashes across his face. He closes his eyes before turning away. 'The academy must be destroyed,' he declares, and loud gasps rumble through the room. Then he points to Dr Dòyìnbó. 'It's the only way to ensure that your terrible legacy ends.'

My gaze swings to Zahrah as horror races through me. *Ọgá Gbénga wants to destroy the Academy of the Sun?* That was never part of the plan. She stares back at me, an equally confused expression on her face. But Ọgá Gbénga isn't finished yet.

'We must protect this nation.' I don't like the look in his eyes as he stares at the Solari gathered in the hall. 'And I see now that Dr Dòyìnbó's Solari cannot be allowed to roam free unchecked.' He turns to Zahrah. 'Round them all up until I decide what to do with them.'

Zahrah straightens instinctively, but her expression is hard. 'No!'

There's a deafening silence as Ọgá Gbénga freezes. Zahrah's voice was a fierce whisper, but the defiance in it is unmistakable.

'Have you forgotten which side you're on, daughter?' Ọgá Gbénga questions through gritted teeth.

Zahrah spreads her hands out in front of her. 'This is wrong! The Solari shouldn't have to pay for Dr Dòyìnbó's crimes.'

Ọgá Gbénga shakes his head. 'I'm not trying to make them pay; I'm trying to protect this country.'

'Careful, Gbénga,' my father says quietly. 'You're beginning to sound like Dr Dòyìnbó.'

Ọgá Gbénga rounds on my father, his eyes flashing. 'What do you suggest we do? Just moments ago, Solari were fighting one another. Do you want to unleash that onto the rest of the country? Onto the world?'

'We can stop the fighting,' I cry. 'We just need to help them see the truth.'

'You really think you can change their minds after so many years under Dr Dòyìnbó's influence?' Ọgá Gbénga shakes his head. 'No, it's too late. You heard what he said – they won't stop.'

My jaw clenches at his stubbornness. 'That's not true. Look at me and Nchebe. Even now, others like Ọ̀rẹ́ and Chigozie have chosen to help us. These Solari have never had a choice before, but we can give them one.'

'It's too risky,' Ọ̀gá Gbénga replies, his voice flat.

'What about you, Daddy?' Zahrah says suddenly. 'Didn't Dr Dòyìnbó train you too?'

Ọ̀gá Gbénga flinches as her words hit him square in the face. I'm impressed. I've never seen Zahrah stand up to him like this before, and I can tell Ọ̀gá Gbénga doesn't know how to handle it either.

'That's not relevant,' he replies in a dismissive tone.

'Yes, it is,' Zahrah insists. 'For so long I've thought of the academy and the Solari in it as my enemies. I believed they were different from us because of everything you've told me.' Zahrah's voice grows stronger, ringing out across the room. 'But I've got to know Onyeka and Nchebe, and they're just like us. The only difference is that you've protected the Òmìnira while Dr Dòyìnbó has been using the Solari.'

Ọ̀gá Gbénga grimaces before looking around the room. 'That doesn't change the threat they represent.'

I cross my arms over my chest. 'They're not a threat. They're kids!'

'I know you want to protect Nigeria, Gbénga,' Papa says.

'But that's what Dr Dòyìnbó claims he's been doing and he got it wrong. The future isn't his to change or control, just as the future of the Solari isn't yours to decide.'

'Please,' I plead, rushing down the stage. Papa is right behind me as I come to a stop in front of Ọ̀gá Gbénga. 'Give me another chance to speak to the Solari. I know I can get them to understand.'

'I'm sorry, Onyeka. The risk is too great.'

Anger blazes through me. *Why won't he listen?* There's a desperate light in Ọ̀gá Gbénga's eyes, and I realize I've seen that look before. It's the same expression Dr Dòyìnbó wore outside Ogbunike Caves as he revealed his awful plans. I can't believe it's happening again – another adult who thinks he can make decisions for all of us. Ike rises in me and I let it, ready to defend my fellow Solari any way I can.

Then Zahrah steps in front of her father, her hands outstretched. 'If you love me, you won't do this.'

'Zahrah—' Ọ̀gá Gbénga begins.

'No, Daddy!' she interrupts. 'We're Ọ̀mìnira; we fight for freedom.' There's a tremble in her voice, but the rest of her is rock steady. 'This isn't what Mama would have wanted and it's not going to bring her back. If you're taking the Solari, you'll have to lock me up with them.'

Ọ̀gá Gbénga's eyes go wide, and he stumbles back with a slow shake of his head. I can't tell who's more shocked, him or the crowd. There are more gasps and growing rumblings at

247

Zahrah's earnest declaration, Òmìnira and Solari alike unable to believe that she's willing to stand with us, even if it means having to suffer herself.

Time seems to slow down as we all wait to see who will win the battle of wills between father and daughter. Ọgá Gbénga looks haunted, but Zahrah is unmoved, her eyes steady on her father as she wills him to make the right choice.

At last, Ọgá Gbénga comes to a decision and his gaze moves to me.

'This is your only chance. Use it well.'

I suck in a sharp breath as Zahrah throws herself into her father's arms. Ọgá Gbénga looks bewildered for a moment, but then his body relaxes and his arms close round her.

I say a small prayer under my breath and return to the podium on my own to face the expectant faces watching me. *This is it.*

'Over forty years ago, Dr Dòyìnbó set in motion his plan to take control of this country . . .' I begin.

I explain how Dr Dòyìnbó was the first Solari and how he's been influencing the Councils ever since. I tell them about the disease and what really happens to Protectors. I inform them that my father and aunt have created a cure. I reveal the truth about Gbénga's revolt and the Òmìnira.

'We can't trust any of this. They're our enemies,' someone yells. It's Fa'idah, and her eyes are wide with fear.

Professor Sàlàkọ́ clears his throat loudly. 'I can confirm

everything Onyeka has said. I am Òmìnira, and I've been living with you all for years now. If I'd wanted to hurt you, I could have done so a long time ago.'

The whispers increase at this new piece of information.

'Dr Dòyìnbó has got this far because he's kept us fighting each other,' Adanna adds. 'He couldn't risk the Òmìnira revealing his lies.'

'We're all Solari, no matter what Dr Dòyìnbó has said,' I add. 'We'll be stronger if we work together.'

I go on to tell them that Dr Dòyìnbó has been hunting us since we left the academy and how he kidnapped my best friend to blackmail us.

'He wouldn't do that.' Another shout, this time from one of the house prefects.

Several heads around him nod in agreement, and I sneak a peek at Dr Dòyìnbó. The pleased smile curving his lips fills me with dread. *Is he right? Is it too late to get through to the Solari?* I shake the thought away. I can't give up.

'Yes, he would,' Òrẹ́ shouts. 'And I helped him do it.'

Ẹni steps up beside him. 'We both did.'

'Yeah, you did,' yells an outraged voice, and I follow it to find Cheyenne, flanked by Hassan. 'And you ate my food too.'

With this final revelation, the mood in the room begins to shift. The academy students all know Ẹni and Adanna have serious beef between them. There are too many witnesses for the Solari to easily dismiss now.

'We don't have to be weapons,' I say, pressing my new advantage. 'We can choose to be something else. Something better. Nigeria is our home, and it's time it knew we existed.' My chin lifts. 'We've lived in the shadows.' Then I point to Dr Dòyìnbó. 'Lived his lie for too long. But now I choose truth.' I stare out at the gathered crowd, a blaze of hope burning in my chest. 'What will you choose?'

A small silence follows my loud cry, and the blaze flickers. Just as I think I've failed, that our words weren't enough, a lone, strong voice pipes up from beside me.

'I choose truth!'

I turn to find Zahrah, shoulder to shoulder with me.

'Me too,' Adanna says from her position in the crowd.

'And me,' Niyì yells.

'I dey four,' Hassan calls out, followed by Cheyenne, even though technically she doesn't count.

Then an enthusiastic cry comes from my left, and I follow it to find Uche and his lizard, a big grin on both their faces. He punches a fist into the air.

'The Òmìnira are with you!' he shouts, and it's echoed by the others surrounding him.

But the remaining Solari are still silent, a hesitant fog of uncertainty blanketing them. A heavy weight settles in my belly. Then Òrẹ́ steps forward, Ẹni right beside him. They look at each other and nod as one.

'We're with you.'

Their friends follow soon after and it seems to trigger something as more Solari speak up until a symphony of voices chorus their pledge back at me. What's left of the weight in my stomach dissolves completely. It's replaced by a joy so sharp that I feel as if I could battle a whole army with it. I'm glad I don't have to.

I stare at the strong walls surrounding us. Green-and-white banners hang proudly from them, a flaming sun blazing bright from the centre. Beneath them sits the motto of the academy: *We serve Nigeria*.

For too long, this has been our militant response whenever Dr Dòyìnbó demanded it from us. But no more. Now, we'll serve each other. We'll serve the truth. Then I remember another question Dr Dòyìnbó used to ask us often, and only now do I understand its true importance. I take a deep breath.

'Who are we?' I bellow.

'We are Solari!'

The answering sound is a thundering roar that fills the whole room and follows me as I leave the stage. It echoes like a battering ram, shattering the last of Dr Dòyìnbó's lies and tearing through the division he created. We'll created a new legacy for ourselves, one that's completely our own.

I face Dr Dòyìnbó, locked once again in Papa's grip, and he looks smaller somehow, like a shrunken version of his former self.

'It's over,' I tell him. 'We're no longer yours to command.'

Dr Dòyìnbó gives me a sad look. 'I did what needed to be done. Now this country and all of you are lost.'

'You're wrong,' Papa says in a quiet voice. 'It's you that's lost. We saw you as a father figure, but no loving parent would do what you did.'

Dr Dòyìnbó doesn't say a thing, but a dawning look of horror enters his eyes as my father's words find their mark. But it's too late.

'Take him away,' Papa says as he hands Dr Dòyìnbó over to Emem. 'Professor Sàlàkọ́ will show you where the captured Òmìnira have been held.'

Before I know it, I'm surrounded by the rest of Nchebe, along with Cheyenne, and she wraps me in a hug.

'You did it!'

'I knew you could,' Adanna adds as she muscles in too.

'You do well o,' Hassan says to Zahrah, giving her a friendly bump on the shoulder.

She stares at him, but I see the small smile trying to peek through her stern expression.

'Can we please never do anything like that again?' Niyì says as Cheyenne and Adanna release me. There's a small cut over his left eye.

I nod back wholeheartedly, touching my damaged strands. I hope we never have to.

'Oh no,' Cheyenne gasps, her horrified eyes following my hand. 'What happened?'

I shrug. 'It's just hair. I'll be fine.'

I realize for the first time that it's finally true. We're all going to be fine. Then Papa returns and my friends step back to give us some space.

'What happens now?' I ask him.

Papa takes my hand and gives it a small squeeze. 'We live, nwa m nwanyi. That's all we need to do.'

In his eyes, there's a promise of what's to come, and it's beautiful.

CHAPTER
TWENTY-NINE

'Onyeka!'

I smile, warmth flooding me as Chigozie's voice cuts across the loud hum of the busy atrium.

It's been six months since the showdown with Dr Dòyìnbó, and the atrium is once again packed with students, hurrying to their next class. Light filters through the tinted solar glass windows, casting a shimmery haze over everything and bathing us in a golden hue. The white polo shirt and green shorts that form our new uniform blaze brightly in its glow.

Heads turn at Chigozie's raised voice, eyes following my progress as I make my way over. I barely notice though, my attention fixed on the grinning girl in front of me.

'How far?' I say with a smile.

'You're wanted in the principal's office,' she replies.

My head tilts in surprise, and a stray chunky twist flops

across my Second Sight. My hair is finally growing back, and I tuck it into place to join the rest of the twists that cascade down my back in a blue-black waterfall of hair.

'What's happened?' I ask concerned.

Chigozie shrugs and I push back the urge to question her further. I know better than to keep our new principal waiting. With a quick wave, I turn and head towards the main office, my brain trying to work out why I've been summoned.

My eyes drift towards the main staircase, searching automatically for the massive digital screen. But the rankings list and houses are gone, and along with it, the competitive atmosphere that used to stalk the academy and everyone in it. The patriotic banners are also no more. Propaganda – that's what Adanna called it as we watched them being pulled down and replaced instead with colourful artwork by local artists.

My feet clack loudly along the hard floor as I hurry towards the office, but I can't help but pause as I pass the huge baobab tree. The names carved into the rich brown bark that winds around its thick trunk are a new addition. They're a reminder of every Solari who has died serving Nigeria ... serving Dr Dòyìnbó's lie. It's also a reminder that we must never let it happen again.

I haven't thought about Dr Dòyìnbó in a while. After he was arrested by the Councils' special security officers, he was quickly tried in a secret court and found guilty of human rights abuses. Papa's worried that Dr Dòyìnbó is still hiding secrets, but he reckons he'll spend the rest of his life in prison.

With a quick shake of my head, I continue on my way, striding past the tree. I turn into a wide corridor on my right. It's empty except for the two littles heading towards me.

'That's not fair, Muhammad,' Ṣeun cries in a petulant voice. 'You know you're not allowed to teleport when we're playing hide-and-seek.'

Muhammad stares at her totally unbothered.

'You're just annoyed because I won,' he says.

I ignore them as a message alert from Cheyenne pops up on Second Sight. After she was kidnapped, my parents had no choice but to tell hers about the Solari population. It was the only way they could explain the fake message and why Cheyenne had missed art camp. Uncle Dàpọ̀ and Aunt Tèmi were livid at first, but they eventually came around. Uncle Dàpọ̀ even decided to move the whole family back to Nigeria, and he's just got a big part in a major Nollywood film.

Just as I'm about to open the message, a collision warning flashes across my vision. Muhammad is so busy crowing to Ṣeun, he hasn't seen me, and I barely manage to sidestep his hover wheelchair.

'Muhammad —' I begin in warning.

'Sorry,' he calls out sheepishly, before he goes right back to taunting Ṣeun.

The sound of their bickering follows me, even as I round the corner, and a lightness fills me knowing that they won't ever have to worry about the sickness. They get to have the future that so many Solari before us never did.

When I reach the principal's office, I knock once then enter. Aunt Naomi's attention is fixed on her virtual fibreglass desk, her fingers flying over the holographic icons as she works. The office looks completely different. With all the heavy wooden furniture and pictures removed, it feels lighter and more welcoming. The bookcase and secret room are gone too. Adanna and I insisted it be sealed up, and no one was about to argue with us.

'You called for me?' I ask. My voice is hesitant, but I can't help it.

Aunt Naomi looks up then. 'Thank you for coming, Onyeka,' she says in a soft voice.

After the epic showdown with Dr Dòyìnbó, we weren't sure what would happen to the academy. Would the Councils close the school, or try and lock us up like Ọ̀gá Gbénga considered doing? In the end, they decided to keep AOS open because so many of us are still young. No one wanted to risk enrolling untrained Solari into regular schools, and my father and Ọ̀gá Gbénga were adamant that we shouldn't remain Nigeria's dirty secret. Though no one can decide when or how to reveal our existence.

Now the Òmìnira have joined us, the school is bigger than ever. We needed a head teacher we could trust and one who also understood what it means to be Solari. Aunt Naomi was the perfect choice and a chance for a fresh start. It's also why we changed her title from head teacher to principal.

'Is everything okay? Has there been another fight?' I ask.

'No, no, nothing like that. I didn't mean to worry you.' My body relaxes. 'I called you here because I received a message from your parents. They'd like you to go home for a visit next weekend. I wanted to check with you before I approved it.'

I nod as relief fills me. Papa is an Elder on the Lower Council now, and he and Mum live together in a nice house in Lagos as they've decided to give their marriage another go. So much has changed in just a few months. My life back in London before I discovered I was Solari feels like a dream, but now I'm fully awake. It's great having Papa around; he makes Mum happy and we're getting to know each other properly. Though it does mean I have another person telling me what to do all the time.

I'm even enjoying my classes and I'm making lots of new friends. AOS now has day boarders, but I'm a full-time boarder because of Nchebe. We have to be ready at short notice in case any new Solari pop up. I go home at weekends and during the holidays, though.

'Yeah, that's fine,' I reply.

Aunt Naomi gives me a small smile. 'You shouldn't worry about the fighting. It's going to take a while for the academy kids and the Òmìnira kids to settle down, and for Solari to truly become one. I'm quite pleased with the progress we've made over the last few months. There hasn't been a fight in at least a week.'

I nod again. There actually was a fight yesterday, but Nchebe are so good at breaking them up now that Aunt Naomi doesn't always hear about them.

Something niggles at the back of my mind, and I wonder if I should tell her. Then I shake the thought away. Aunt Naomi's got enough on her plate trying to set up the Solari Force with Ọ̀gá Gbénga and Papa.

After graduating from AOS, Solari no longer have to become Protectors or join any of the armed forces. We're free to decide our own futures now. Instead, the Solari Force will be tasked with protecting Nigeria and its citizens from any Solari who might decide to create trouble in the future. It's our way of taking responsibility for the potential harm our powers could cause. It's totally voluntary, but Niyì has already signed up for the four-year training programme.

'I'm hoping a peaceful transition at the academy will help ease the Councils' worries about how Solari will fit into society once the secret is out,' Aunt Naomi says.

I doubt it somehow. The Laamu-EzeOba has agreed to reveal our existence, but the Councils are taking their time deciding when. Adanna reckons they're worried about how the world will react to finding out about Solari. I don't say this though.

'Do you know when they're planning on telling everyone?' I ask instead.

Aunt Naomi shakes her head. 'These things take time and a lot of diplomacy, but I believe things are moving along. I'm sure your father will be able to fill you in when you see him next week.'

I doubt that too. Papa never tells me anything that's going on with the Councils. Aunt Naomi stands and gives me another smile, but I recognize the dismissal in it. Just in time too, as the talking drums signalling lunch sound. My stomach growls along to the driving rhythm. I really hope there's asaro on the menu. Niyì hates it, but I love the chunky yam pottage, especially when it's sweet.

The canteen is buzzing as usual when I enter. Several Solari stop to say hi, and I pause by Òrẹ́ and Ẹni's table to chat for a few minutes. Then I spot the rest of Nchebe at our regular spot. Hassan, Niyì and Uche are bent over their food, laughing, while Adanna is playing with Zahrah's hair. It's orange now, and she's growing it out again. Adanna's eyes lift, zeroing in on me straight away. Even in an emotionally crowded room of clashing sounds and scents, she can always find me. She waves, and I make my way over.

CHAPTER THIRTY

'This dance battle better start soon o,' Uche says before I've even sat down. The agama lizard on his shoulder nods as if it agrees. Then Uche stands suddenly and begins moving his legs in an awkward shuffle. 'I've been practising my legwork all week.'

'You and that lizard need more practice,' Adanna says with a roll of her eyes. 'Why do you all like to dance in the middle of the canteen anyway?'

'Why do you take everything so seriously?' Uche replies undaunted. 'You should try and relax small, small.' He pats the lizard on the head gently. 'Ganiru thinks you should try having some fun, eh?'

Adanna crosses her arms. 'I am relaxed.'

I push down the laughter bubbling up in the back of my throat. No day is complete without Adanna and Uche getting into an argument. Though, to be fair, they're usually harmless. I quickly point to Uche's empty chair beside Zahrah.

'Sit yourself and Ganiru back down,' I command with a grin.

Uche groans but obeys anyway. I take the seat beside Niyì before greeting everyone.

'I dey enjoy dis asaro well, well,' says Hassan, digging his fork into the bright orange mountain on his plate. I eye it with envy.

'Chai, do you ever stop eating?' Niyì replies with a grimace.

Hassan laughs, giving him a close-up view of the food in his mouth. I watch them with a smile. Then Adanna turns to me. Her locs are pulled up in a complicated style I helped her create.

'Chey texted me,' she says, tapping Second Sight. 'She wants to know if the sleepover is still on this weekend?'

So *that's* what her earlier message was about. I totally forgot the sleepover was this weekend. Chey's a full boarder at her school too, but we have a sleepover here at the academy every two weeks.

'Sure,' I reply. I'm not going home until the week after anyway.

Suddenly, Uche gives me a broad grin. 'I hear you had to go see Dr Uduike . . . Ooh, someone's in trouble.'

'You do know the principal is her aunt, right?' Zahrah reminds him.

Uche's smile dips into a pout that makes him look like a fish. 'Why are you like this?'

Zahrah just shakes her head before taking a bite of her meat pie.

'Everything okay?' Niyì asks me.

I nod and explain about my parents. I also tell them what Aunt Naomi said about the Councils.

'What do you think it will be like when everyone finally finds out about us?' Zahrah asks.

Niyì shrugs. 'I think it will be a bit chaotic at first.' Then he looks from me to Zahrah. 'You probably won't see much of either of your dads for a bit.'

Zahrah and I share a look. Ọ̀gá Gbénga is also on the Lower Council, and Zahrah spends most weekends with him.

Adanna tugs gently on one of Zahrah's orange braids. 'Maybe you can join Nchebe properly then?'

'We're going to be on billboards and stuff,' Uche says, excitement filling his voice.

'We go be popular well, well! E go be like we dey inside film,' Hassan joins in.

Adanna rolls her eyes. 'More like a horror film,' she says in a sour voice.

'There you go again,' Uche says with a groan.

'Fine.' Adanna sighs, then her voice goes all weird and high. 'The world is totally going to love us, everyone will follow us online, and someone will put all our faces on expensive T-shirts.'

The table goes completely quiet, then we all burst out laughing at how ridiculous she sounds.

'What about you, Onyeka?' Uche asks when the laughter finally dies down.

I shrug. I don't know if the Nigerian people, or even the rest of the world, will accept us, but it almost doesn't matter. We're Solari and nothing can change that. As long as we remain united and remember who we are.

'I think we'll be fine,' I finally say.

Just then, an Afrobeat song pours out of the speaker system, signalling the beginning of the dance battles.

'Are you people coming or not?' Uche calls at us as he moves towards the dance area.

I grin at my friends. He's right. It's time to have some fun because we've more than earned it. I get up and join him, showing off my shoki moves. Soon, the others join us, even Adanna, and together we dance, letting the joy of the beat, the hope in the rhythm and the power of the lyrics flow through us. It unites us in a single, beautiful moment that nothing can touch or ruin.

My room is dark and quiet as I let myself inside. Adanna stayed behind in the canteen with the others and I'm alone. I switch on the light and jump as a tall figure steps forward.

'Hello, Onyeka.'

'Papa!' I squeal, recognizing his deep voice. His arms open and I rush into them. 'What are you doing here? I thought I wasn't seeing you until next week?'

'I'm here on official Council business.' He pauses. 'We've just found a new Solari.'

I step back and blink at him. *A new Solari?* There hasn't been one since ... well, since me. I stare at Papa, trying to understand what this means for the Councils and especially for the academy. Though, from the look on Papa's face, I'm guessing it's not great.

'Where are they?' I ask. 'Are they here already?'

Papa shakes his head. 'That's why I came. The Solari isn't in Nigeria. He's in England – Bristol to be precise.'

Bristol? My mind races as I try to make sense of my dad's words. But I can't. *How in solar did a Solari end up in Bristol?*

'I don't understand,' I finally say.

'We don't have the full picture,' Papa says, rubbing his face. He looks tired. 'But we do know that we need to get him out of England right now before there's a diplomatic incident. The Solari Force isn't operative yet, so Nchebe must go.'

'B-but,' I stutter. 'We're not ready. We're still training.'

Papa places a gentle hand on my shoulder, his eyes alight with a faith that settles my nerves.

'You *are* ready,' he says in a firm voice. 'It's time.'

PRONUNCIATION
GUIDE

Adanna	Ah-dan-a
Dòyìnbó	Doh-yin-bow (as in hairbow)
Ẹni	Eh-nee
Fọlákúnlé	For-la-koon-lay
Gbénga	Gb-ain-ga
Hassan	Ha-san
Ike	Ee-kay
Nchebe	Nn-chay-bay
Niyì	Nee-yee
Ògá	Or-ga
Òmìnira	Oh-mee-nee-ra
Onyeka	On-yay-ka
Òrẹ́	Or-reh
Sàlàkọ́	Sah-la-core

Tópẹ́	Tor-kp-eh
Tósìn	Toh-sin
Uche	Oo-chay

GLOSSARY

Agbalumo A popular fruit. Also known as the African star apple.

Akara A type of fritter made from beans and often eaten for breakfast. Also known as beanballs.

Asaro A pottage made from yam that is boiled until it's tender and then cooked in a blend of peppers, tomatoes, onions, palm oil and seasoning.

Ayo A board game of Yoruba origin, similar to mancala.

Chin Chin A sweet, crunchy snack made from fried dough.

Eba A staple dish in Nigeria made from garri flour (grated casava). It is often eaten with soups / stews such as efo riro.

Efo Riro   A stew / soup commonly made with spinach, palm oil, stock fish, crayfish and red bell peppers. It is often accompanied by solids, such as pounded yam or fufu. It can also be called efo.

Hausa Koko   A spiced porridge made from millet and often eaten for breakfast in the northern parts of Nigeria.

Milo   A malted chocolate-flavoured powder, typically mixed with milk, hot water, or both, to produce a popular drink.

Oba   Means 'ruler' and is the title given to kings in Yorubaland.

Oga   A Yoruba word that means 'boss' or 'senior'. It is often used as a form of address in Nigeria.

Pepper Soup   A very spicy soup, packed with meat and flavour. Popularly sold at Nigerian relaxation spots and used as a remedy for a cold.

Pounded Yam   Made from boiled yam that has been mashed or 'pounded' into a soft, semi-solid state. A staple dish in Nigeria, it is often eaten with soups / stews, such as efo riro. It can also be made using yam flour.

Puff Puff	A sweet snack made of leavened dough, deep fried in oil. Similar to a doughnut or beignet.
Shoki	A popular afrobeat dance.
Suya	A popular street food of spicy meat (beef, chicken, offal, etc.) roasted or grilled on skewers or whole.
Talking Drum	A small drum shaped like an hourglass. When struck in a specific way, it can mimic the tone and sound of human speech.

NIGERIAN PIDGIN ENGLISH

Nigerian Pidgin English or 'Pidgin' is a language spoken widely across Nigeria and much of West Africa in various forms. It is a mix of English and local languages, which enables people who do not share a common language to communicate. It originates from the late seventeenth and eighteenth centuries, during the transatlantic slave trade. It was originally used by British slave merchants and local African traders and then spread to the rest of the West African colonies. Though not currently recognized as an official language, it is estimated that up to 75 million people in Nigeria use it today.

Common words:

Abeg	Please
Am	Replaces 'him' or 'her' in a sentence
Belle	Stomach

Chai	An exclamation, used to express surprise, grief, disappointment, or anger
Chop	To eat
Dat	That
Dey	To be, or to be in the process of doing something
Dia	There
Dis	This
Don	Have, has or had
E	It
Ehen	An exclamatory sound with different interpretations depending on the context used
Fit	Suggests an ability to do something – can
How far?	What's up? / hi
Make	Signifies that you are going to do something – let
Na	Is / was
Na Wa	Exclamation used to express surprise or shock
O	Usually used at the end of a sentence. An exclamation often used to reiterate a point, answer a call, or used to confer agreement
Oya	Let's go – often used as a call to action (originally a Yoruba word)
Sef	Too / also

Small chops	Finger food / snacks
Wahala	Trouble / problem. Though, depending on the context, it can also mean 'yes' or 'no problem' (as in, 'No wahala.')
Wan	To do, or want to
Wetin	What
Wey	That / which

ACKNOWLEDGEMENTS

When I first started writing about Onyeka and her unique journey, I never could have imagined where this story would take me. I am so grateful to all the people that have made these books possible, and all the readers who have taken Onyeka into their hearts. Thank you from the bottom of mine!

It truly takes a village to send a book out into the world, and I'd like to thank my own hardworking one. To my agent, Claire Wilson. Your support and guidance have been invaluable, and you already know I think you're a superhero. Also, thanks to Safae El-Ouahabi and the rest of the team at RCW.

To my editors at Simon & Schuster, Amina Youssef and Kate Prosswimmer. You are the iron that sharpens these stories, and I'm so excited to continue this journey with you. Thank you also to Rachel Denwood and Ali Dougal for your continued faith in the world of the Solari. Thank you also to the detailed eyes of my copyeditor, Veronica Lyons, and proofreader, Deborah Balogun.

To the rest of my team at Simon & Schuster, Olivia Horrox, Dan Fricker, Laura Hough, David McDougall, Loren Catana, Sophie Storr, Maud Sepult, Theo Steen, Jane Pizzey and Dom Brendon, a massive thank you. Onyeka could not have soared the way she has without all of your passion and hard work. Thank you also to the team in the US at Margaret K. McElderry Books for bringing the series to such glorious life across the pond.

Thank you, Brittany Jackson, for another stunning cover. The image of Onyeka and her epic hair is truly iconic thanks to your brilliant vision and artistry. I know many readers were drawn to the series because of your amazing work.

I remember vividly my visit to the recording studio to hear the incomparable talent that is Nneka Okoye voice Onyeka for the first time for the audiobook. Thank you, Nneka, for breathing life into the story.

I am beyond grateful to all the amazing booksellers who helped readers discover Onyeka and the Solari. Special thanks to Waterstones and their amazing booksellers, such as Emma, Mary and Robbie, as well as Blackwell's, Afrori Books, Books & Kulture, A New Chapter Books, This Is Book Love and The Bookworm Cafe. Thank you also to all the educators and librarians who have championed this series, and all the bloggers like Nicci Rosengarten, Tom Griffiths, Scott Evans and Fabia Turner who took the time to shout about it.

Thank you also to Queen Egemba, Millie Anozia and Ògúndélé Gbénga Paul for your help with the various languages in this book.

To everyone in the writing community who has supported me, said such kind things about these books and made me feel so welcome, thank you. Thank you also to my amazing friends for your continued support and love.

And, finally, to my phenomenal family, for the prayers, babysitting, listening ears and gentle wisdom. I love and appreciate you all. And the biggest thank you to Goziam, Elizabeth and Rebekah for all the sacrifices you've made so these books could be birthed. You are my world and I adore you.

This book is dedicated to God, without whom none of this would be possible. Thank you, Abba, Father.

Tọlá Okogwu is a British-Nigerian author, journalist and hair care educator. Born in Lagos, Nigeria, but raised in London, England, she holds a bachelor of arts degree in journalism. Having spent several years exploring the world of blogging, hair care and freelance writing, she finally returned to her first love: fiction. She is the author of the Daddy Do My Hair? picture book series, as well as *Aziza's Secret Fairy Door* under the pen name Lola Morayo. *Onyeka and the Academy of the Sun* is her first middle-grade book. Tọlá now lives in Kent with her husband and two daughters. An avid reader and lover of music, she's also a sucker for melted cheese.

Learn more at tolaokogwu.com.

HAVE YOU READ?

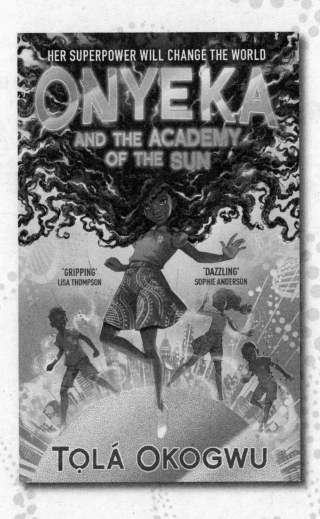

Don't miss out on reading the third

ONYEKA

adventure

COMING
MARCH 2024